Out *of a* Pale Blue Sky

Tim Davidson

Tim Davidson lives in Clifton, Bristol and is a retired solicitor. He is married to Maddalena, a teacher, who comes from the Veneto region of Italy, and they have two grown-up sons, Thomas and Nicholas. His interests include reading, walking, classical music and opera.

By the same author:

The Bloomsbury Manuscript. A novel
Music critic Hugo Belcher is a charming rogue who, forever short of money, plans to marry a wealthy young heiress. Meanwhile, Sandra Grisewood, a bright working class girl, moves to London where she hopes one day to realise her dream of becoming an opera singer. Two hundred years before in late-eighteenth-century Prague, music teacher Antonin Vasylicek, another charmer, flees to London to evade his creditors and escape a scandal. Their separate lives are, however, inexorably linked in various ways, not least the coming to light of an opera score based on Goldoni's comic play *Il Servitore di Due Padroni* (*The Servant of Two Masters*).

Time For Another? A collection of short stories within a novel
George, Tom, Desmond and the Colonel are regulars at the back bar of the Sloop Inn. They delight in hearing stories related by visitors to the bar whom they have managed to engage in conversation, stories of love, infatuation, surprise and deception, tales with happy endings and tales ending in catastrophe. The regulars themselves also become involved in a disturbing story of their own...

Out *of a* Pale Blue Sky

Tim Davidson

STEPHEN MORRIS

First published in 2016 by Stephen Morris
www.stephen-morris.co.uk
T: 0208 946 8705
E: smc@freeuk.com

©Tim Davidson

ISBN 978-0-9930554-4-7

British Library Cataloguing-in-Publication Data
A catalogue record for this book is available from the British Library

Designed by Stephen Morris, smc@freeuk.com www.stephen-morris.co.uk

CHAPTER ONE

It is famously alleged, probably falsely, that Beethoven described the first four notes of his Fifth Symphony as 'Fate knocking at the door'. In my case, fate wasn't so polite as to knock, it just barged into my life, uninvited and unexpected.

'Damn,' I said to myself, out loud, as I extracted a charred piece of toast from the grill, burning a finger in the process. This was the second time, that morning that I'd managed to burn the toast. Most people, I know, would probably use a much ruder word to express pain and annoyance, but I like the word 'damn'. It has a nice solid, emphatic ring to it.

'Damn, damn, damn' I repeated.

Without being too fanciful, I might, in retrospect, have regarded this incident as a mini-portent of all the awful events that were about to follow, a tiny harbingerette of doom. As it was, I consigned the blackened slice of bread to the bin, ran my injured finger under the cold tap for a second or two and thought no more about it.

Just as I had resumed my seat, the telephone rang. It was my good friend and colleague, Mike Hailey, suggesting that I might like to accompany him the following day on 'a little adventure', as he put it.

'Not bloody likely! Not another of your bloody adventures!'

'But this one is only a gentle little stroll in the Malvern Hills not a trek in the high Andes! And they're forecasting a nice day tomorrow, and neither of us is on chapel duty. Come on, William, you'll enjoy it! '

'The answer is no!' I replied firmly. 'The last time you persuaded me during the Easter break, against my better judgement I might add, to accompany you on what you called an adventure, we got hopelessly lost in the Welsh mist somewhere in the Black Mountains and I thought we'd never be seen again. Gentle stroll, my arse!

Knowing you, I'm sure it would turn out to be an arduous all-day romp suitable only for those who have undergone an advanced course of military training. Tell you what, though, Mike, how about a few beers and a curry this evening?'

'Can't do this evening, I'm afraid – got a date!'

'What with Tina again?'

'Of course. Well, if you won't come on the walk with me, too bad! See you at the staff meeting on Monday evening, if not before. Perhaps, if Dr. Babble doesn't detain us for too long with one of his long, meandering speeches, we might manage a drink or two afterwards.'

Dr. Hugh Drabble, or 'Babble' as he was dubbed in the junior staff common room, was the Headmaster of Hanfield Manor School, a minor public school where Mike and I were employed as teachers. I taught History and Mike Physics.

Dr. Drabble's nickname arose partly, of course, as a play on his surname but mainly because of his tendency towards verbosity and an infatuation with the sound of his own voice. This would often result in staff meetings lasting rather longer than they needed. He was, to be fair, a decent man, though one who often appeared remarkably unworldly or, as Mike put it, perhaps a little unkindly, 'a complete prat'.

Monday's staff meeting, however, seemed mercifully a long way off – Now, it was only Saturday morning, and I was enjoying – at least trying to enjoy, when not interrupted by the phone ringing or the toast smouldering – a leisurely breakfast in my small kitchen, whilst languidly pondering how I might spend the rest of the day.

Since there was a sixth form outing to London that day to visit the V&A, my Saturday morning classes had been cancelled and there were no classes on Saturday afternoons. Further, like Mike, I was not required for evening supervision and had been excused chapel duty for the Sunday morning communion service, so I had a rare free weekend with no school duties, not at least, until Monday morning.

I was in a good mood. The end of term was just a few weeks

away. Soon it would be the Christmas holidays.

Mike and I were both in our early thirties. We had joined the school staff in the same term some years before and struck up an early friendship. Mike is one of those active, sport-loving, out-of-doors sort of people and was forever trying to inveigle me into taking part in things he calls 'adventures' or 'challenges'. I'm all for novel experiences, of course – attending an opera at La Scala in Milan for the first time, for example, or visiting a famous Bordeaux chateau for a wine tasting – but adventures involving discomfort, undue risk or strenuous exercise are not my thing at all, and frankly life involves too many challenges of one sort or another, as it is, without deliberately looking for more of the damn things. I had no great wish to risk my neck white-water rafting or abseiling down tall buildings; I felt no desperate urge to scale some distant mountain peak; I harboured no burning desire to travel the length of the ancient Silk Road across the steppes of Central Asia on a motor scooter or whatever other perilous undertaking dare-devils, like Mike, think it might be fun to try.

In all other respects, though, Mike and I agreed on most matters and shared the same likes and dislikes. Along with Geoff Mitchell, an English teacher roughly the same age, we were known by our colleagues at school as 'the Young Fogey Brigade' as our view of life, habits, dress and way of speaking were seen by some as more characteristic of an older generation than that to which we belonged. The opinion of our fellow teachers, though not entirely fair, was at least partly justified, though the school's urbane senior classics master, Eustace Petherick, sometimes referred to Mike and Geoff as 'the Thinking Man's Lads'. Whatever the case, we enjoyed our reputation for being different and sought to play up to it whenever the opportunity arose, if only to wind up our contemporaries.

Hanfield Manor is situated on the western edge of the Cotswolds between Stroud and Cheltenham. The main school building is a late-nineteenth-century mansion and was originally built as an orphanage in a hideous Gothic horror story style, at the expense of some

Victorian philanthropist. The architect, who conceived of this monstrous edifice, must surely have possessed a well-developed sense of humour or, on reflection, perhaps not. The building lent itself, however, to transformation into an independent boys' boarding school quite successfully and lay in an attractive semi-rural setting. Though the school might have been something of an educational backwater, it was a pleasant enough place in which to work, my colleagues, for the most part, were a convivial bunch of souls and there was about it an easy-going, clubbable sort of atmosphere.

I lived in a small studio apartment created out of the loft space of an old flour mill converted into flats on the outskirts of a large, straggly village within five minutes drive of the school. Small it may have been, but it was a snug little garret and very conveniently located in what was now a quiet, leafy area. It suited me very well. I enjoyed teaching, too, and flattered myself that I had a natural gift for it.

I'm not particularly ambitious and, all in all, I was more than content with things as they were. One might put it this way: if anyone could be found to deliver a eulogy at my funeral and was unable to summon up anything else to say about me other than 'William Wilkins was a good teacher, enjoyed the company of his friends, but otherwise led a quiet life', I would rest happy in my grave.

But *Life is full of surprises* and *you never know what's just round the corner,* as they say – whoever *they* are who persist in trotting out these clunking clichés and trite truisms – and I had not the faintest premonition that bright morning that my cosy existence was very soon to be utterly shattered by a series of tragic and terrible events which, as *those they* would say, came completely *out of the blue.*

CHAPTER TWO

Since Mike had an assignation that evening with Tina, I had decided to treat myself to a takeaway from the nearby Indian restaurant, The Cotswold Tandoori. Tina, Mike's current inamorata, worked in the school office as secretary to the bursar, and must have been about twenty-six or seven-years old. She was, I thought, a singularly attractive young lady. One has to say, though, that she was a bit of a flirt and was rumoured to have enjoyed what the urbane Mr. Petherick referred to as 'unseemly liasons' with several younger members of staff in the short period of her employment with the school. It was now Mike's turn, as he put it, 'for a twirl on the amorous roundabout'.

Tina had yet to flutter her eye-lashes in my direction, an unlikely event, I thought, for I'm by nature a quiet, self-effacing sort of chap, and I very much doubted that a girl like Tina would take much interest in me. Ah well, too bad!

As I waited for my takeaway to be ready, I slipped across the road for a swift pint at the White Bear, the village pub on the opposite side of the main road. By a happy chance, I found, propping up the bar there, Geoff, the other member of the so-called Young Fogey Brigade or Thinking Man's Lad. He bought me a beer and we talked about Mike, wondering where he had taken Tina for dinner.

'Likely as not some cheap pizza parlour, knowing Mike.' I said.

'Oh, I don't think Tina would let him get away with that.' Geoff replied 'Tina's the sort of girl who likes the high life; she'll probably insist that he takes her to one of those posh places in Cheltenham mentioned in the foodie guides – It'll cost him a fortune!'

'Hope so...'bout time his wallet got a proper airing – serve the bugger right!'

'Absolutely! Got time for another one, William?'

'No thanks, Geoff. Have to go and pick up my takeaway.'

❖

I had only just got back to the flat and was in the process of opening up the cartons containing my Balti Chicken and saffron rice, when the 'phone rang. It was my mother. She sounded extremely agitated.

'William, I've some terrible news...it's your father...'

'What, what is it, Mum? What is it? tell me!'

'When I came home from the supermarket this evening, I found him slumped over the desk in his study. He tried to say something to me but he...he couldn't speak. I phoned for an ambulance right away and they came very quickly. The ambulance man said that he'd suffered a serious heart attack...'

'Oh, my God! ... But, but how is he now? Is he conscious? Where have they taken him? Which hospital?'

'Oh William... He...he died in the ambulance on the way there...'

❖

The death of my father Theo – so very sudden and unexpected – was devastating. At first I simply could not properly take it in.

I loved my father dearly. Perhaps because I was an only child, we were very close, and I felt his loss deeply. It left a gaping hole in my life where once he had been. I have often heard people who have lost a parent or close relative say that a part of them too had died and that it was the end of an era in their lives. Now I understood what they meant.

Intensely proud as I was of my father's achievements, it was comforting for me to read a glowing obituary which appeared a few days after his death in *The Times*:

> Theo Wilkins was an art dealer much respected not only by his
> peers and but by academics, collectors, curators and many

others connected with the art world. Although remarkably catholic in his tastes and knowledge of many genres and periods, he established a formidable reputation for his specialist knowledge of Italian painting of the eighteenth century. Indeed, he was often called upon to give advice upon matters of authenticity.

Theobald Arthur Wilkins (Theo, as he was always known) was born on the 21 September 1948 in Canterbury, the second son of Arthur John Wilkins, by profession, an archaeologist, and his wife Heather, a primary school teacher.

Wilkins studied at Edinburgh University where he obtained a first degree in History of Art, and thereafter, as a young man, worked for several galleries in London before opening a small gallery of his own in Bath with the little money left to him by his father.

After some ten years in Bath which saw the growth of a successful business, he moved to Orchard House, a substantial Regency property in Cheltenham. The ground floor comprised his new gallery, known as The Orchard Gallery, while the rest of the house served as the Wilkins family home. The Orchard Gallery flourished and it was perhaps inevitable, given his growing reputation, not only as a dealer but as an acknowledged expert in his field, that he soon opened a gallery in London where he had many influential contacts and many of his wealthier clients were based. For much of his career, he divided his time between the London and Cheltenham galleries, though Orchard House in Cheltenham would always remain his home.

The whole of the top floor of Orchard House was converted into a private gallery for Wilkins' own art collection which, unsurprisingly, focused particularly on works within Wilkins' specialist field, eighteenth-century Italian painting. To be a serious collector of masterpieces of the period by the likes of Tiepolo and Canaletto, for example, would require the resources of a multi-millionaire, though a painting of the Zattere in Venice, which Wilkins bought at auction in Paris was later attributed to Bernardo Bellotto.

There were of course many fine lesser known painters of the time and it is works by such artists that Wilkins, with an infallible eye for future collectability, had acquired over the years. His collection, though, also comprises works by more notable painters, including a portrait of a rather rotund English aristocrat on the grand tour by Pompeo Bastoni and a fine set of four paintings depicting scenes of domestic life in eighteenth-century Venice by Pietro Longhi, sometimes referred to as the Italian Hogarth. The latter set of paintings was not, however, acquired by purchase, but was bequeathed to Wilkins under the will of the late Sir Bernard Skelton, a wealthy industrialist and art collector, who had been a life-long client and friend.

Wilkins frequently opened his private gallery to art historians, researchers and others with a particular interest in Italian painting of the eighteenth-century period and often generously lent paintings for public exhibitions at museums and art galleries in Britain, The United States of America and other countries in Europe.

Wilkins' interests were not confined to fine art. He enjoyed fly-fishing, was a talented pianist and built up a fine collection of seventeenth- and eighteenth-century Delftware.

Two years ago, Wilkins sold his business to the well-known Mayfair firm of art dealers, Maurice Beckman & partners, but he continued to be retained as a consultant until his death at home last Saturday. He is survived by his wife, Marcia, and their only child, William, now a teacher at a private school for boys in Gloucestershire.

Only in his late sixties, my father had seemed in perfect health: he was still at work several days a week, often travelling to London.

Naturally, I didn't want my mother to be on her own in such awful circumstances, and, there and then, decided to drive the short distance to Cheltenham to be with her. Indeed, I spent the rest of the evening there and stayed the night. It was the least I could do.

The next morning, at breakfast, I found her quite withdrawn, which was most unusual for her. She looked pale and barely uttered a word – a consequence of shock, I supposed at the time, but there was though another reason which I was later to discover. In any event, she seemed quite content for me to take sole responsibility for the tedious tasks which always require dealing with when someone dies.

I rang the school early on Monday to advise what had occurred and spoke to Matthew Richards, the Deputy Head, as Dr. Drabble was – happily perhaps – unavailable. Mr. Richards, a sensible and kindly man, told me not to bother to come into school. There were not many classes that week as the boys were doing their end of term exams and he would arrange for Derek Pearson, my senior colleague, to take the few classes still on my schedule. Someone else would take over the exam sessions which I had been supposed to invigilate.

Freed from school responsibilities, I spent the next few days in a frenzy of activity: registering the death, talking to undertakers and the local vicar to make the funeral arrangements, and ringing round a list of old friends of my father as well as a longer list of remoter relatives of the sort to whom one sends Christmas cards but with whom one only tends to speak in the event of a death in the family. Then there was, of course, the current manager of the Orchard Gallery, father's solicitor, his bank and so on to be contacted.

In the few conversations I was able to coax my mother to have with me, we had agreed upon a simple funeral service, for relatives and close friends only, at the local parish church. I felt sure that this is what my father would have wished. The idea was that a memorial service would be arranged at a later date.

CHAPTER THREE

On the Thursday of that week, I drove down to see my Uncle James, known always as Jimmy, at the residential care home in Weston-Super-Mare where he lived. I had thought it best to visit him in person to inform of my father's death rather than to write or telephone.

My father had two brothers and a sister and there was a wide age spread between them – Uncle Jimmy, whom I'd come to visit and who had spent his working life as a shipping agent, was the oldest, more than ten years older than Dad. Health considerations had forced him to move into a care home. Aunt Mildred was the next child of the family, five years younger than Uncle Jimmy. She was married to a retired naval officer with two children, my cousins Tom and Kate. Finally there was Uncle Charles, in his early sixties and the youngest of the four siblings. He was the sales manager of an electrical good business near London. Uncle Jimmy was a bachelor and was always known to Tom, Kate and I as 'the Good Uncle', while Uncle Charles who had been married three times and had no children, at least not by any of his wives, was known as 'the Bad Uncle'. Auntie Mildred, charming, but absent-minded, was known to the whole family as 'Silly Milly'.

Poor Uncle Jimmy was now in very poor health and suffered from moderate dementia. He clearly recognised me, though, and when I told him about his brother's death, his shoulders dropped, he bowed his head and sobbed for a few moments. We, or rather he, talked about his childhood life in Kent where he, his brothers and sister grew up. Every episode was prefaced with the words 'You remember when...', but of course how could I? I wasn't born. I played along, though, as best I could, simply nodding in agreement without interrupting him.

At last there was a break in uncle's stream of reminiscences and I felt it was good time for me to go. As I rose to my feet, he looked up at me with smile.

'It was very kind of you to come, dear boy.' He said, 'Do give your father my fondest love, and please tell him to come and see me soon, very soon.'

❖

I drove away in the rain in the gathering darkness, arriving home tired and depressed. Although I didn't really feel very hungry, I thought I ought to have a light snack and I made my way to the kitchen. There, on the work surface near the microwave, was the day's post which I had brought in that morning but not yet opened.

There was the usual quantity of junk mail, a letter from the opticians advising me that I was due for an eye test, and an envelope with the school crest embossed on it. That would be the Headmaster, I thought, with condolences upon my father's death. It was, though, rather more than that. I sat at the kitchen table, opened the letter and began to read its contents, which, characteristically of Dr. Drabble, took some time to come to the point:

Dear *William*

I was very sorry to learn of the death of your father. Please accept my sincere condolences and those of the Chairman of Governors. Please would you also convey our sympathies to your dear mother.

These sad circumstances make my task in writing to you today, as I must, all the more difficult.

You will be aware, no doubt, that pupil admissions in this academic year are well down on the figures for last year. The substantial shortfall in income, coupled with rising annual expenditure, has placed a severe pressure on the school's finances which the Governors believe has now become unsustainable.

Hanfield has always enjoyed a close relationship with Mallory College; close, indeed, in more ways than one as their grounds adjoin our own. Confidential discussions between our respective School Governors have been ongoing for many months. These discussions have recently borne fruit and it has been agreed that our two schools will merge. The legal formalities may take some time to complete before we officially become one school, but practical arrangements will be put into effect from the beginning of next term.

One can see useful synergies arising from this merger. While Hanfield is a boarding school for boys, Mallory is a day school which also admits girls. The merged school would be co-educational and offer places for both boarders and day pupils, thus broadening our base by appealing to a wider range of prospective parents. Linking our two sites would provide ample room for expansion, and there are ambitious plans for a new science block. Finally, of course, the size of the school would give us a greater market presence.

To be frank, though, I had hoped that our financial situation might improve with the passage of time, and allow us to retain our independence. Hanfield, however, lacks the endowment income and resources enjoyed by some of the larger schools in the private sector, and the Governors were of the view that, to safeguard our future viability, we cannot afford to miss the opportunity that the proposed merger with Mallory College offers us.

Mallory, as you may know, have two experienced teachers of History who will take over our History courses, joined by our own Derek Pearson. I'm afraid, however, there is no position currently for a further History teacher. One of the objects of the merger, you will appreciate, is to achieve economies of scale, and we cannot afford to be overstaffed. The two existing teachers at Mallory and Derek Pearson are all senior, both in terms of age and length of service, to yourself and, in the circumstances, I am truly sorry but the school has no alternative but to terminate your employment with effect from the end of this term.

You will, of course, receive, as your contract provides, a term's salary in lieu of notice in addition to your full redundancy entitlement. The Bursar will be writing to you shortly with details.

I do hope you will attend the final school assembly on the last day of term as The Chairman of Governors would like to make a small presentation to you in recognition of your loyal service and the great contribution you have made towards the life of the school.

I wish you every good fortune in securing a new position worthy of your talents.

With deep regret,

Yours sincerely,

Hugh Drabble

Headmaster

As I digested, with mounting horror, the momentous contents of the Headmaster's letter, I was overcome with anger and in a fury I flung the glass of supermarket Sauvignon, which I had just poured myself, at the kitchen wall.

Just to add to the misery when I swept up the shards of broken glass from the floor, I found that the glass I had thrown was not one of my every-day variety but one of a pair of Waterford crystal wine glasses which my father had given me as a birthday present. This seemed somehow cruelly symbolic of all that had happened, and it was all I could do not to weep with self-pity.

God knows what other damage or injury I might have caused to myself or the flat had not the telephone rung. Thankfully, it was my old friend Mike Hailey who had come to my rescue. He had heard the news, of course. Tina had found a copy of the Head's letter on the Bursar's desk and tipped him off. I was not the only one to lose his job. Foreign languages were also targeted for cuts and two other teachers, whose jobs were being taken over by people from Mallory College, had been given their marching orders...not that this was much consolation to me.

'Plainly you're in need of a stiff drink, followed by a few more!' Mike said firmly 'Geoff and I will meet you at the White Bear around eight – see you there.'

CHAPTER FOUR

My father's funeral took place twelve days after his death on a cold, miserable and wet Friday afternoon.

'Bad Uncle' Charles delivered an amusing and touching eulogy at the funeral service, which I must say raised my spirits a little. He was on very good form, and though he might be a bit of a rogue so far the fair sex is concerned, I had always found him good company. Rogues usually are.

After the service, we held a reception at Orchard House which passed off reasonably well, though 'Silly Milly' had much too much to drink and kept bumping into people, colliding with the furniture and giggling.

The only damper on the occasion was my mother who – normally the life and soul of the party – sat by the fireplace in the drawing room and hardly spoke a word to anyone. Again, I put this down to shock and sadness, understandable in the circumstances... but that was not the full story, not by a league.

As proceedings drew to a close and people started to collect their coats and edge towards the door, Dennis Thrupp, my father's solicitor and old friend, came up to speak to me.

'William, I need to see you soon about your father's Will...When would suit next week?'

'I'm tied up at school on Monday and Tuesday, but I could do late afternoon on Wednesday, say 4.30.'

'That would be fine. I'll see you then.'

CHAPTER FIVE

So it was that on Wednesday of the week following my father's funeral, I duly attended, as arranged, the offices of Messrs Thrupp, Sanderson & Co, solicitors, in the centre of Cheltenham for my meeting with the good Mr. Thrupp to discuss the Will and winding up of the estate. My mother had told me the night before that she didn't feel up to it and was happy for me to attend the meeting on my own.

I was in for another unexpected shock, more than one in fact.

'Did your father tell you he had changed his Will, William?' Mr. Thrupp asked

'No, my father was always quite secretive about his affairs. He never talked to me about his Will...or for that matter much about his investments or money, at least not very often and then only in rather vague terms.'

'I see...Knowing your father as I have done over the years, not just as a client but as a friend, that certainly has the ring of truth about it.'

Mr. Thrupp paused to clear his throat before continuing 'Well, It is perhaps fortuitous that your Mother was unable to come along this afternoon. It would have been rather embarrassing for you. You see, your father made a new Will about two weeks before his death, revoking his previous Will and leaving his entire estate to you as his only child and appointing you and me as his executors. I don't know whether or not your mother is aware of this.'

'Good God! You mean he cut her out of it altogether?'

'Yes, that is the case.'

'But why on earth' I continued. 'What possibly could have made him to do such a thing, I mean cut my mother out?'

'Well, naturally I questioned his motives, but he was quite

adamant about it. He said that your mother was capable of looking after herself.'

'But that's preposterous! She would have to go back to work full time.'

'Quite so...and it is most unlikely, even if she did so, that her income would be anything like sufficient to support the lifestyle to which she is used. Of course, I advised your father that your mother would almost certainly have a valid claim on the estate on the basis that the Will failed to make adequate provision for her.'

'I see, but there would be no need of that, I mean for mother to make a formal claim, I would, of course, allow her stay on free for the rest of her life at Orchard House, and naturally I would make sure that she is properly provided for out of my inheritance. There should be plenty of...'

Mr. Thrupp put up his hand to stop me in mid-flow.

'I'm afraid it's not quite as simple as that, William. You see Orchard House had always been treated as an asset of the gallery business and thus went with the deal when the business was sold to Maurice Beckman & partners two years or so ago.'

'But I...I don't understand...It's my parents' home, and they continued to live there after the sale went through.'

'Let me explain the position, William. Under the terms of the deal for the sale of the business, your father was given a five year consultancy agreement, a not uncommon arrangement in deals of this nature. Your father was, of course, beyond normal retirement age but the agreement only committed him to attend on a part-time basis.'

'I knew that he remained as a consultant with the business after the sale, but Dad never told me on what terms.'

'Well, the agreement provided for a very generous income in return for your father's advice and continued part-time involvement, together with bonuses depending on the annual profits and a high rate of commission on sales for new business he introduced. I did advise him to take out a Term Insurance policy to cover early demise or incapacity, but unfortunately, it seems, he didn't do so. Now, coming to the matter of Orchard House, the agreement also contained a special clause allowing your father – and mother of course – to remain in occupation of the residential parts of the house free of rent and maintenance cost whilst the agreement subsisted. But, of course, this arrangement automatically terminated when your father died.'

'You mean to say my mother will have to leave the house?'

'I'm afraid so, yes, though the agreement does allow a six month period of grace to vacate after termination to allow time for your mother to find an alternative residence.'

'I see...Well, Beckman must surely have paid a handsome price for the business, so I can at least buy a nice flat for my mother to live in?'

'Again, I'm afraid things aren't quite that simple.'

'Why on earth not? What's the problem now' I said, unable to resist a hint of irritation creeping into my voice. Why do lawyers, I thought, always have to make such heavy weather of things?

'Please bear with me and allow me to explain, William. The gallery business was very high-geared...'

'High-geared?'

'Well, the business operated on a high level of debt. As a result of the financial crash in 2008, the business, like many other businesses of this size, especially those trading in luxury goods, suffered a sharp decline in profits and cash-flow difficulties. The bank borrowings increased substantially as a result. Indeed, it was lucky that your father was able to persuade the Bank to agree to increased facilities as the business might not otherwise have survived.'

'But I recall my father saying that the business had recovered well from the recession.'

'Yes, the business picked up and returned to profitability, but the level of debt remained very high. Suffice it to say that when the business was sold to Beckman the value of the stock, both in

Cheltenham and London, together with the value of the house only barely exceeded the total of the outstanding bank loans and overdraft. The London gallery itself was held on a lease at a very full rent and had little premium value.'

'You mean to say that the business wasn't worth anything?'

'Well not exactly. Beckman paid an upfront premium but only a quite modest sum. Of course there was substantial goodwill value, as we call it, but that was entirely associated with your father personally and his knowledge, expertise and connections. That's why, indeed, Beckman retained him as a consultant. So the real value of the deal to your father lay in the very generous consultancy terms, which I have already mentioned. But all that came to an end, as I've explained, with your father's death'

'But, surely my father was a wealthy man?'

'Well, that all depends what you mean by that. I'm afraid to say that there is very little actual cash available. In fact, when your father died, he was running quite a sizeable personal overdraft at his bank.'

'Oh, my God, I can't believe it!'

'Look, William, your father enjoyed the finer things of life. When he travelled, even when he was not on business, he always stayed at the best hotels and dined at the best restaurants, he was a regular opera and concert goer and he fished twice a year on the most exclusive salmon rivers in Scotland. But, above all, he was, as you know, a collector of fine art. Instead of investing in treasury stock, pension policies, Glaxo shares or whatever, he bought paintings and many of those must surely now be worth a great deal of money.

'Your father effectively regarded his art collection as his pension fund, and, on expiry of his consultancy, he intended to sell up his paintings except, no doubt, for a few special favourites. With the money realised he would discharge any remaining debts and buy a decent home for retirement in place of Orchard House. The remainder sensibly invested, would provide a goodly income to live on for the rest of his and your mother's lives. That was his game plan.

'Sadly he died before that could happen, but the paintings

remain – they are your real inheritance, William!'

'Yes, I see.' I said, rather lamely.

'William, I know that all this must be quite a lot for you to take in at one go, and I'm sorry things are not more straight-forward, but your father was an unusual sort of man...'

Sensing that the meeting was over, I rose somewhat shakily to my feet, still a little taken aback by all that I had heard. Mr. Thrupp looked up at me with an odd sort of expression on his face. He seemed a trifle embarrassed..

'Is there something else you wish to tell me, Mr, Thrupp?' I asked.

'I regret to say there is. I've wrestled in my mind as to whether I should say anything to you, but I think you have the right to know...'

'Well, what is it?' I asked a little nervously. Surely, I thought, there couldn't be yet a further surprise in store? There was.

'The real reason your father altered his Will was not because he believed your mother had sufficient earning capacity as he first suggested, but because he had just found out that she was having an affair with another man.'

'What?!' I cried out.

'I'm afraid so. Your father said that he was contemplating divorce. Had he not passed away so suddenly, no doubt, you would have found out anyway. That is why I thought it proper that I should tell you.'

CHAPTER SIX

I drove home from the meeting with Mr. Thrupp, trying to come to terms with all that he'd told me. Most of all, though, I was angry with my mother, more angry than I'd ever been before about anything. I had had not the slightest inkling of her affair until Mr. Thrupp informed me of it, and neither my father nor my mother had said anything to me which might have indicated that something was amiss between them. In fact, I had only spoken to my parents once or twice very briefly on the telephone during the past four weeks, and had not found the time to visit Orchard House as I'd been busy at school.

I should, I know, have waited until I'd calmed down a bit, but I didn't – In a fit of rage, I phoned my mother the moment I stepped through the door of my flat before even troubling to remove my coat. It was to be a brutally short conversation.

'I've just come from Mr.Thrupp. Father changed his Will before he died' I said curtly.

'Yes, I know. He told me he was doing so.'

'And you know very well why he changed the Will, don't you?!...You betrayed him with another man!'

'William, you've always taken your father's side, but for once please listen to me. Let me explain...'

'There's nothing to explain. There's no excuse...You bloody betrayed Dad after all these years. That's all there is to it. You're loathsome. I shall never forgive you!'

I slammed the phone down, and paced up and down the room. I have always liked to believe that I was good at keeping my feelings under control, keeping the upper lip properly stiff and all that, but anger surged through me like a little stream converted by a sudden flash flood into a raging torrent. It was some while before the anger level began to drop.

As the emotional waters receded, a sense of remorse at the way I'd spoken to my mother gradually crept over me and, with remorse, came reason and, with reason, understanding.

Dad was at heart a kind man, but he was inclined to be moody and during his moody phases, he often became sullen and uncommunicative. He could not always have been the easiest person to live with.

Then there was the age disparity – Mum was sixteen years younger than Dad. She had taken a part-time job at the gallery in Bath while she was studying at the Bath School of Art and Design for a design diploma. Even allowing for my natural bias as her son, I can honestly say that my mother, in middle age, was an extremely attractive woman, and, as a student, one need only to look at photographs taken of her at the time to see that she was then, by any standards, a stunning beauty. I imagine my father, as many a man might, became besotted with her and she in turn was probably flattered by the attentions of an older man. In any event, romance blossomed and they were married even before she had completed her diploma. Her father, a G.P. in Dorset, and her mother understandably opposed the match, at least until they discovered that she was already pregnant. Pregnant with me.

More significant perhaps than the age difference was the difference in temperament. Dad was not shy but neither was he a gregarious or flamboyant character in the manner of some of his peers. He possessed a brilliant mind, was exceptionally well-read and enjoyed intelligent conversation with people he liked. He hated small talk and loathed parties. In contrast, while sharing Dad's love of art and music, Mum was an outgoing, extrovert sort of person; a good socialiser; a doer not a thinker; tidy, efficient, a brilliant organiser; always on the go.

She continued throughout her life to help Dad first at the Bath gallery and then in Cheltenham right up to the sale of the business to Maurice Beckman, after which she took a part-time job at a local antique shop. Although I'm quite sure Mum and Dad loved each other, there was an inevitable brush of temperament. There were frequent rows over silly things, and it is true that I usually took my father's side, unfairly in retrospect. Everyone who knew my parents well could see that their relationship was not always an easy one, everyone that is but me. Looking back on things now, though, it was obvious and had become more so in recent years – the sarcastic comments, the awkward silences, the looks, the body language.

What Mother had done in taking up with another man was wrong, but in all the circumstances perhaps not entirely surprising: how could I really blame her?

It was too late to phone her again that night, but I resolved to do so in the morning and to adopt a more conciliatory tone. She must be assured, too, that I would help with her relocation and that I would always, of course, see to it that she was well provided for. Even if there was a shortage of cash now, there should, I thought, be plenty of money around when the art collection had been sold.

Early the next morning before school, I tried to phone her, but there was no reply. I remembered that this was one of the days she was at work and sometimes, I knew, she would leave home quite early to have a coffee somewhere on the way. In the circumstances, I decided to wait and call again in the evening.

I duly called again when I got in from school, but there was no reply on the landline and I tried Mother's mobile, got no response from that either but left a message for her to call me.

❖

The following day, Friday, was the last day of term, and, with some reluctance, I drove into school for the final school assembly.

A letter had been sent to all the parents about the teachers who were leaving and about the proposed 'merger' with Mallory College, so none of this came as a surprise to either staff or pupils at the assembly. The atmosphere, though, was rather subdued – most unusual for an end of term assembly before Christmas.

The Headmaster made a vain attempt to raise spirits with one of his long rambling speeches, trying without much success to persuade everyone what a great future lay in store.

Finally the Chairman of Governors, Sir Giles Pendleton rose to his feet to speak. Sir Giles lived with his wife and family at his ancestral home, Pendleton Court, Little Pendleton, a village not far from the school. He was a bluff, red-faced caricature of a country squire. Indeed, he was also Chairman of the parochial church council and a Justice of the Peace. He barked rather than spoke, and unfortunately got me mixed up with John Wilson, a junior French teacher, who was also one of those who were leaving the school as a result of the impending merger.

According to Sir Giles, poor John Wilson could apparently reel off the names of every ship that had taken part in the battle of Jutland, whilst I was able to sing the Marseillaise better than the captain of the French rugby team. At the end of this pathetic oration, each of the teachers who were leaving was presented with a pair of cheap-looking cufflinks, bearing the school crest, which I have absolutely no intention of wearing. What a waste of time!

CHAPTER SEVEN

On the way out of the school – for the last time, as I could hardly believe it to be – I met Wanda Parker, who used to be the Headmaster's secretary. She was divorced from her husband, the CEO and main shareholder of a successful property development company, and had obtained a very substantial divorce settlement. She had no need to work after her divorce but had continued to help out with secretarial work in the school office on a part-time basis, probably because she was a jolly soul and simply enjoyed the company

Wanda, who must have been forty or so, was a large lady in every sense – a large woman possessed of a larger than life personality. She was always heavily made-up and dressed in a manner which I can only describe as provocative. How she managed to squeeze her ample frame into the sort of garments she wore was one of wonders of nature. In her way, though, and if your preference is for ladies of a fuller figure, she was certainly not unattractive.

Mike maintained that Wanda had a taste for younger men. Whether this was true or not, salacious gossip, or perhaps just wishful thinking on Mike's part, I had then no means of knowing.

'Bit on the plump side.' I observed in The White Bear one evening when her name came up in conversation.

'Plump, plump? Hardly the mot juste, William. Good God, the woman's *baroque*, positively *baroque.*' Mike replied, savouring the words as he spoke them. 'Why, if Wren or that other bloke Vanbrugh had designed women instead of churches and palaces, they'd all have looked like Wanda!'

I had just reached the staff car park and was about to get into my car to drive away when Wanda approached me.

'Hello, William' She said 'So sorry to hear that you're leaving us, and about your poor father, too. I'm sorry we didn't get a chance to talk at the funeral...'

'Well, it was very kind of you to come, Mrs. Parker.'

'Not at all. I particularly enjoyed meeting your uncle Charles, such a charming man, and he spoke so well about your father.'

'Yes, I thought so too.'

'Look, William, I'm having a little drinks party this evening at home. Would you like to come along? I've asked Geoff Mitchell too. I'd love to see you, and do please call me Wanda.'

I wasn't exactly in a party mood, but couldn't think on the spot of a plausible excuse to decline the invitation.

'Er, yes, Mrs.Parker, Wanda, I mean, thank you very much; I'd love to come.'

'Good, good...about six-thirty, then.'

I had heard nothing from my mother in response to the message I'd left on her mobile and I phoned several times during the course of the day, each time with no result, the last time just before I set out for Wanda's party.

Wanda lived in a beautiful old house of mellow Cotswold stone in the delightful small town of Painswick, and I must say she certainly knew how to put on a good party – excellent canapés and a splendid winter punch. The trouble was that I had too much of the punch which tasted delicious but was far from innocuous. I don't know what Wanda had put in it but it was pure dynamite, and I began to slur my words.

At about eight-thirty or so, people were beginning to say their farewells and drift away. I found myself standing quite close to our bubbly hostess. Why, I asked myself then in my semi-drunken state, had I ever considered Wanda to be an over-painted, fat trollop...No, no, I told myself, she was beautiful...in fact more than beautiful,...she was absolutely voluptuous!

'*Shplendid* party, Wanda...*musht* be off now.' I said.

'Now William' she purred, sotto voce, moving up very close to me, 'You don't have to go yet, you know, just because the others are going. Why not stay, and we'll have a little supper together, just the two of us?'

Just at this moment, Geoff appeared at my elbow. I think he must have been close enough to catch the drift of what Wanda was saying.

'William' he said, 'I'll give you a lift home. Leave your car here and pick it up tomorrow.'

'But, but...'

'Come along now, William.' Geoff insisted, taking me firmly by the arm. 'Good-bye, Wanda, and many thanks for a really lovely party!'

Geoff led me out of the house and guided me quickly to his car which was parked a little up the road from Wanda's house.

'Geoff' *Ish* very kind of you to give me a lift and all that, but Wanda had invited me to *shtay* for *shupper..*'

'You'd have got more than supper, if you'd stayed, you mark my words!'

'*Sho* what?!' I said, in a slightly belligerent tone.

'I'll tell you 'so what'. You mustn't let on to anyone, though, especially Mike, but I had a little tryst with Wanda once myself. I ran into her in the corridor outside the school office one day and she asked me to dinner the following evening. In fact, it was just after the end of last summer term. I'd had to go into school for a final staff meeting.

'Naturally, I thought there would be others present, but there weren't. There were just the two of us. I must say she had prepared a simply splendid dinner. Wanda got the house as part of her divorce settlement and a fully-stocked wine cellar came with it – her Ex must have been quite a connoisseur. We had some epic wines with the meal and of course I drank too much – lost all inhibitions.

'In any event, we were soon playing footsie under the table. After dinner, we repaired to a comfortable sofa in the drawing room where Wanda cosied up ever closer to me as we sipped our coffees.

One thing led to another, and of course I ended up staying the night, and not on the sofa! What a night, I can tell you!

'The next day, I was due to go off to Portugal to stay with my brother who's got a place there. How I managed to get to Luton to catch my plane to Faro, I just don't know. As it was they'd nearly closed the flight by the time I arrived. I was completely knackered!

'I tell you, Wanda's a man-eater; she hungers after men – she'd have gobbled you up, old chap, eaten you alive!'

'But I should quite like Wanda to gobble me up.' I replied, plaintively.

'And the worst thing' Geoff continued, ignoring my interruption 'was that when I returned from Portugal at the beginning of term, she continued to pursue me...relentlessly. She would wait for me after school in the staff car park – after a bit, I took to leaving my car there and walking out via the playing fields and catching a bus. Then there were the letters and emails. My God, you should see what she wrote in the emails, prose as purple as bishop's cassock! I tell you, William, I've saved you from a dreadful fate, believe me!'

Geoff kindly saw me home and I staggered up the stairs to my flat. There was no message from my mother on the answer phone and I couldn't be bothered to check my mobile which had been turned off all evening. I'll just have to keep trying tomorrow, I thought, before collapsing on the bed and falling, still fully clothed, into a deep slumber.

CHAPTER EIGHT

I had no knowledge of the existence of a man called Gordon Trench nor the slightest connection with him. There was no reason why I should have, and even less reason to know that Gordon was a traffic warden and that on the morning of that day, the last day of term and the day of Wanda's drinks party, he was patrolling the streets of Cocklemouth, a small sea-side town on the Dorset coast.

Gordon was a retired army sergeant, and had taken up the job as a traffic warden partly in order to supplement his army pension and partly to prevent himself from becoming bored during his retirement. The squaddies over whom he took charge during his service in the army all believed that he had applied for the job as a traffic warden simply so that he could go on being a 'right bastard' as he always had been. In fact, Gordon was not so much a bastard as a stickler for the rules, but this was a distinction entirely lost on his squaddies, not to mention the legions of irate motorists with whom his new job brought him into contact.

Shortly after he came on duty that morning, Gordon was striding purposely along one of the roads leading down to the sea front. If it was consistent with his duty schedule, he usually chose this road as the first one to patrol. It was quite a narrow road, and there were only a few spaces on one side of it where parking was permitted.

There was a newsagent about half way along, and motorists often parked illegally on the double yellow lines outside whilst they quickly nipped into the shop to buy a newspaper. If he were patient, Gordon was generally able to catch and ticket at least one motorist and sometimes two. That morning was no exception; the unfortunate driver came hurrying out of the newsagent to remonstrate, but his pleading was to no avail and a penalty notice was duly affixed to his windscreen.

With an air of smug satisfaction, Gordon walked on down the road in the direction of the sea front, humming to himself a melody from a regimental march – the very march, indeed, of the distinguished regiment in which he himself had proudly served.

But what was this? There was another car parked on the double yellows about thirty yards or so further on in the narrowest section of the street. It was badly parked, too, more than 15 inches from the kerb and not even parallel with it. A private car might just be able to squeeze past, but any larger vehicle would find it very difficult at least without mounting the pavement on the other side of the road...and what if it was an ambulance or fire engine?!

This was not simply a case for a penalty notice on its own, Gordon thought. He would wait for the recalcitrant driver to return and give him or her a right good bollocking for lack of consideration - not only inconveniencing other road users but potentially, if the passage of an emergency vehicle were impeded, causing risk to life. With years of experience behind him as an army sergeant, Gordon prided himself on his ability to deliver a good bollocking, one comprising just the right blend of stern admonishment and cruel humour at the offender's expense. This day was shaping up to be a really good day, Gordon thought, and a little smile played about his lips. There was no greater pleasure for him than giving someone a good bollocking when they truly deserved it.

However, as he came up alongside the car, he noticed that the driver's door had not been closed properly and the key was still in the ignition. Judging from these factors and from the careless way in which the car was parked, Gordon's instincts were beginning to tell him that the car may have been abandoned. His first thought was that it had been stolen, but then he saw that there was an envelope on the driver's seat. Opening the car door, he bent down and picked up the envelope to take a closer look. Written on it, were the words: 'Please give this to my son William Wilkins'. This was followed by an address somewhere in Gloucestershire.

The envelope was not gummed down and he could see that it

contained a note. After some hesitation, Gordon decided that he ought to read it. He felt justified in doing so as the note might reveal how the car came to be left as it was, which in turn might have a bearing on his decision as to what to do about it.

As he read the note, his eyes widened, his bristly military moustache stiffened, and his large square jaw dropped in shock and surprise.

CHAPTER NINE

I awoke suddenly in the morning, Saturday, following Wanda's party to the sound of the entry phone bell.

I heaved myself out of bed and went to answer it. Looking at my watch, it was only a quarter past seven. I could have done with another hour's sleep. Bother!

'Yes, who is it?'

'Police, sir... Please may I come up.'

Wondering what on earth this could be about – had there been another burglary, perhaps, in one of the other flats? Perhaps they wanted to know if I'd seen anything. I pressed the entry button for the main door of the block and opened my own front door in readiness. Eventually, a very tall policeman made it up the stairs to the landing outside my flat and I motioned for him to enter.

'What can I do for you, officer?' I asked.

'I'm afraid I have some very bad news, sir.'

'Oh, really?' I answered, nonchalantly. After all, I was getting quite used to bad news by now.

'I think you better sit down, sir'

He said he was very sorry to have to inform me that my mother had taken her own life.

Taken her own life, suicide! I simply couldn't believe it. I found it difficult to take in the story the officer told me and I had to ask him to repeat it all again.

My mother's car had been found abandoned by a traffic warden yesterday morning in a small town on the Dorset coat– in fact, I knew the town the policeman mentioned. It was where my mother had spent her childhood.

As CCTV footage later confirmed, the car arrived quite late in the evening of the previous night. A woman was seen getting out of it and walking down the road in the direction of the sea-front. The same woman was again picked up on camera as she made her way along the sea-front promenade behind the beach in a westerly direction towards the steps leading up to the cliff path.

An elderly man was out walking his dog along the cliff path that evening. He had passed a woman walking quickly in the opposite direction towards the headland. Though it was dark, there was a full moon that night and the man had got a good view of the woman as she walked by. It was the same woman.

The man lived in a nearby former coastguard cottage and often took his dog for a walk at night, but he rarely met anyone else on the cliff path after dark in winter, let alone a woman on her own. Continuing his stroll, but still curious, he turned to look back just in time to see the woman climb over the iron railing on the seaward side of the path and make towards the cliff edge. He was too far away to do anything and, to his horror, he watched as she teetered on the edge for a moment and then flung herself off the cliff into the sea.

As fast as his old legs could carry him, the man made his way back to the spot where he had seen the woman jump just in time to see her body in the water until it was sucked under the waves by the strong undertow for which the area is known. After that, he returned hastily to his cottage on the other side of the headland to telephone the police. A search was mounted, but to no avail.

Nobody of course knew who the woman was until her car was found the next morning by the traffic warden along with the note addressed to me on the driver's seat.

'Dorset police contacted us yesterday afternoon' the officer went on 'and we tried to contact you early yesterday evening but it seems you were not at home.'

'No, I was at a drinks party.'

'I'm afraid, sir, that the police in Dorset kept the original note as it will be required by the local Coroner, but you will, of course, receive it in due course. In the meantime, I have a copy here for you which was scanned and emailed through to us from Dorset...Now, sir, we can arrange counselling, if you wish, and if there is anything else we can do for you now, please don't be afraid to ask... perhaps there's someone else you would like us to contact, for example?'

I shook my head, quite unable to speak.

'Well, sir, in that case, I'd best be going now...Here is the copy of the note and also a list of telephone numbers which may find useful – Police, counselling services et cetera...May I say once more how very sorry I am.'

Placing the copy of my mother's note and the list of numbers on the small coffee table next to where I was sitting, the officer quietly withdrew, gently closing the door after him.

As soon as he had gone, I read the copy of my mother's note:

Dearest William,

It is true that I had a short-lived relationship with another man and I'm not proud of it, but things between me and your father had not been good for some while before his death. He had been more than usually moody of late, and we were barely speaking to one another. I became very depressed and desperately craved love and sympathy. I happened to meet a kind man who offered me the affection and support I so much needed. These are the circumstances in which my relationship came about. In any event, it is over and I've not seen this man since.

Unfortunately, Theo found out about it. We had the most almighty row, during which he said some very unkind things and told me that he was going to cut me out of his will and see his lawyer about a divorce.

William, I had been a loyal wife to your father for over 30 years, except for this one brief lapse. It was surely wrong of

him to cut me out of his Will and threaten me with divorce.
I don't believe I deserved to be treated in this way and I feel
terribly hurt .

I wanted to explain all this to you, but you were plainly
too angry with me to listen. You, too, said very unkind
things.

Now, with Theo's death, I find I have nothing. I feel
rejected by those I have always loved and have never been so
unhappy. I can see no future for myself save one of misery. I
have come to the conclusion that it would be best in all the
circumstances if I now to put an end to my life which can
only become an increasing burden to me and everyone else.

As you know, I spent my childhood in Dorset close to the
sea. The sea is in my blood and, now my life is to end, it is to
the sea that I will return.

I hope one day, William, you will come to understand
and think better of me

With all my love, despite everything,
Mum

I don't know how long I sat slumped in a chair, my head in my hands, hardly able to believe what had happened. When I had first learnt of my father's death, it was enough of a shock, but this was something else. It was a crushing blow, and there are no words to describe the way I felt.

Fortunately the phone rang as I was on the point of spiralling into a dreadful vortex of grief and misery. It was my good friend Mike who once more saved me.

I knew that the day before, after the end of term, he had driven away to Exmoor to stay with his parents who lived in a large and beautiful old house overlooking the River Barle, near Dulverton, from which they ran a hotel business. He had thoughtfully rung me for a friendly chat and to see how I was bearing up. When I told him what had happened since we last spoke, there was silence and I thought we'd been cut off. Mike is not one normally short of words.

After a long pause, he spoke:

'William, you poor, poor fellow, I simply can't find the words to express how sorry I am. This whole thing is like some ghastly Greek tragedy. I'd come straight over to see you if I could, but, as you know, I'm now with my parents down here at Barleton Grange...'

'Yes, I understand' I said, trying not to sound as miserable as I felt.

'Look, William, what are you doing for Christmas?' Mike asked

Good God, Christmas! I'd forgotten all about Christmas, and it was less than a week away.

'Well, I, I don't know really, normally, of course, I spend Christmas with my parents, but...' I replied, my voice trailing off, not quite able to bring myself to complete the sentence.

'Well, you're not spending Christmas on your own, that's for sure! Come down here and spend it with us. It's the least we can do for you.'

'Oh, thank you so much, I'd love to, I really don't know what I'd do otherwise, Kill myself probably! Are you really sure, Mike?'

'Of course, don't be silly. I suggest you come on Christmas Eve. I'm sorry I can't ask you before but the place is full now. We close, though, on Christmas Eve until the 5 January so then we'll have plenty of room for you.'

'That would be lovely, Mike. It's very kind of you!'

'Good, then, that's settled. I don't suppose your old banger runs to a satnav, but I'll send you some directions before you come'

CHAPTER TEN

It never rains but it pours as they, those *they* again, like to say.

Monday morning and I knew that there was something I needed to do; I should have done it before over the weekend, but I just couldn't face it. Since my mother's departure, Orchard House would have been left vacant. Given her state of mind, goodness knows, I thought, how she would have left the place. My Father's art collection was all there, my inheritance! I would, I realised, have to make arrangements as soon as possible to put everything into safe storage, but pending this, I needed to make sure the house was fully secure.

In the light of all that had happened, it would be a painful experience to go there. I could only barely remember my early days in Bath. Orchard House was my real childhood home, a house so full of memories for me, but now it would be a sad and lonely place.

It was with a heavy heart that I drove over to Cheltenham that morning.

The residential part of Orchard House has two entrance doors, one at the front on the main road, next to the gallery entrance, the other at the back of the property. It was the latter that my parents normally used. The rear was accessed by means of a private lane between high walls, serving both Orchard House and several adjoining properties. At the rear of Orchard House, there was a double garage and an iron gate. Next to the gate were a post box and a bell with an intercom for visitors to announce themselves. A gravel path, beside an attractive patio garden, led from the gate to the back door of the house.

Parking my car on the verge by the side of the lane, nothing seemed out of order. The gate into the garden was unlocked, but it usually was, and in any event would have been easy to climb. I had always thought this was a bit of a security risk and was surprised that my father had done nothing about it. Still, I had no immediate cause for worry, but as I walked up the path, I somehow began to sense that something was amiss, and when I got to the door my worst fears were confirmed. The door had plainly been forced. It was badly battered, there were splinters of wood on the ground, the door frame had been smashed, and the lock, which also showed signs of damage, no longer held the door shut and bolted. I gave it a push and entered the house, noticing as I entered that the alarm system control panel appeared also to have been tampered with.

A small passage by the side of the kitchen led directly into a hallway where a winding staircase led up to the floors above.

With mounting concern, I rushed upstairs to the top floor, my father's private gallery. For security, there was a heavy metal door at the entrance to the gallery, but it had proved no obstacle to the intruders who had savagely jemmied it open. The whole collection of paintings was gone. I could scarcely believe my eyes.

The gallery also housed my father's collection of old Delftware and all that had gone too.

I managed finally to pull myself together enough to phone the police. They told me to stay where I was and that an officer would be with me as soon as possible. I must say they were very prompt. About twenty minutes later, a burly police sergeant arrived. He tut-tutted a bit, spent some time examining the back door, had a cursory look around the house, made a few notes and issued me with a 'crime reference number'.

As he left, he said rather cryptically 'There's a bunch of art thieves about' adding, but a bit late in the day so far as I was concerned, 'Got to watch out!'

After the policeman had gone, I thought I would go round to the front of the property to see the manager of the gallery, Jack Beale. Jack had been my father's loyal assistant for many years, and after the business was sold to Maurice Beckman's outfit and my father became a part-time consultant, they appointed Jack manager of the Cheltenham operation. He had attended my father's funeral but obviously had not heard about my mother. He was very shocked and when I told him about the theft, he could hardly believe it. He had not heard or seen anything.

'The police said something about there being a gang of thieves about.' I said

'Well, they were right' Jack replied, 'but not just any old thieves – there have been a number of high profile thefts from country houses, including a couple near here quite recently. Police suspect they are the work of a gang of highly professional international art and antique thieves. They have been warning collectors and people in the trade to take additional precautions.'

'My God! But how would they have known the house was empty?'

'Professional gangs like this do their research well and they know just what to look for. They find out about private collections by making discrete enquiries, pretending to be dealers or collectors or whatever. It's very likely that the boss of the gang knows his stuff well...probably himself a bent dealer. Once they've chosen their target, they keep watch, often employing a team of local 'scouts', and judge the best time to make their move. They've got the whole business down to a fine art, if you'll forgive the pun, believe me.'

'But how do you know about all this?'

'Well, a squad from the Metropolitan Police specialising in art theft have been called in to investigate the spate of country house thefts, and a senior officer from the squad came to see me about a painting, part of a collection, stolen from a house near Cirencester. Normally, speaking the loot is taken up to London or to the continent or even the United States, but this particular painting was of a local scene, not of enormous value, and the police thought that the gang might try to dispose of it to a gallery in Bath, Stow or Cheltenham...The officer who came to enquire was a very nice bloke; we chatted for quite a bit and he explained how professional gangs like this operate.'

'Yes I see, but I wonder why they didn't burgle your gallery while they were about it.'

'Well, it's true we do have one or two nice things here but nothing to compare with the rich pickings in your father's part of Orchard House. Also, we have just spent a lot of money upgrading our security here, it's all really 'state of the art' now and we have the most sophisticated, tamper-proof alarm system on the market. It's like Fort Knox compared to the rest of the building. Why bother, when next door there were plums much riper and easier to pick?!'

'Yes, I suppose so.'

'Look, William, you should make sure the investigation into this crime is handed over by the local constabulary to this specialist squad from London. They know what they're doing...Incidentally I have a schedule somewhere in my office of all your father's paintings; he wanted me to prepare a valuation for insurance purposes. He could have done it himself, of course, but it needed to be independent. It should be bang up to date. I'll look it out and email a copy to you. The police will certainly want one and the insurers too.'

After thanking Jack and providing him with my email address, I returned to my father's study in Orchard House to phone Dennis Thrupp who obviously needed to be informed. He was after all a co-executor of the estate.

I sat down at my father's old desk. It was only then that the full horror of the situation finally came home to me. For some reason, images of the four little paintings of Venetian life by Pietro Longhi, bequeathed to him by his old friend Sir Bernard Skelton, floated into my mind, and I found it difficult to hold back the tears. It was some while before I managed to compose myself sufficiently to dial the number of Mr.Thrupp's firm.

As it happened, he had been trying to contact me with condolences on my mother's death of which he had just heard. When I told him about the theft from Orchard house and my conversation with Jack Beale about the gang of international art thieves, there was a sharp intake of breath.

'I'm absolutely at a loss for words, William.' he said 'The fates really seem to have got it in for you. This is all so awful. I'm very sorry. I'll do anything I can to help.'

'Thank you.'

'William, I think the good Mr. Beale is quite right that we need to make sure that the local police refer the case to this specialist unit. Look, I'll have a word with them for you, if you like, and see to it that it happens.'

'That would be good of you, yes...and I'll email you with a schedule which Jack said he could let me have. Apparently, Dad asked him to carry out a valuation for insurance purposes. The police will obviously want that...Incidentally, I don't know who Dad's insurers are.'

'Well, I know the insurance brokers he used because I recommended them to him. I'll have a word with them and let you know...'

As I drove home from Cheltenham, I dwelt upon my present circumstances.

Only a few weeks ago, I had two loving – at least, I had thought to be loving – parents, who lived in a beautiful house which I regarded as my real home which I had believed they owned and which one day, in the distant future, I would inherit; I had a job as a teacher from which I derived great satisfaction and which paid me a reasonably decent income; life was good and my future seemed secure.

Now I had lost both my parents, my mother in the most tragic of circumstances; the house turned out not to belong to the family at all; my inheritance had been stolen, and I had lost my job into the bargain.

The bottom had fallen out of my world as *they* would say, no doubt, if *they* were me, and indeed *they* might well have added: *and that's the understatement of the century!* But the bottom had even further to fall, as I was soon to discover.

CHAPTER ELEVEN

When I got home in the early afternoon, I found, that Mr. Beale, as good as his word, had emailed me the schedule of my father's art collection, and I lost no time in forwarding it on to Dennis Thrupp.

After that, I ate a rather limp cheese sandwich, bought the day before, which I found in the fridge, and set to work, without much enthusiasm, on preparing a CV to send off to schools and colleges in the search for a new job. I didn't get very far with it, though, and in any case I thought there was little point in sending anything out before Christmas. So I abandoned the task and took a little nap instead in my armchair. I don't know how long I slept, but I awoke with a start to the sound of the telephone ringing. I was beginning to dread answering the phone now, especially the landline, in case it brought me news of some fresh tragedy or disaster, though it would be difficult to see what more could conceivably occur. If the last weeks had been akin to the unfolding plot of some tragic opera, surely the singers had now taken their final bow and the curtain had fallen. I wasn't prepared to bet on it, though.

Nervously, I picked up the phone. It was Dennis Thrupp calling to update me. He had, of course, some bad news.

'William, I had a word with the insurance brokers after we spoke this morning, and I'm afraid I have to tell you that your father's insurance has lapsed...'

'What?!'

'Apparently, he had received a renewal request through the brokers but thought the renewal premium was too high and had asked them to come up with an alternative quote from another insurer. This they had done, but the prospective new insurers were insisting on a condition requiring certain additional security measures to be taken. Your father said he'd consider it, but despite several reminders he failed to reply before he died and the original policy had by then lapsed.'

'Oh, my God!' But this is absolutely terrible. I can't believe it.'

'Yes, I'm sorry – it's a truly awful situation, but I've spoken to the local police and they have promised that the case will be referred to the specialist team who were investigating the other art thefts.

After the call ended, I spent a little while sitting with my eyes closed contemplating my situation in the light of the latest revelations.

It took me sometime to take in the full enormity of it all. My father's entire precious art collection, not to mention his Delftware, had been stolen and it appeared now that the theft wasn't even covered by insurance. If Dad had a fault, he was inclined to be a bit parsimonious and, though he never talked about the specifics, I knew he hated paying for things like insurance where he could see no immediate benefit and he wouldn't have liked spending money on extra security measures either. But allowing himself to become uninsured, that was unforgivable! The fact was my inheritance was gone! Though the police would no doubt do their best, I had little real hope that anything would ever be recovered.

No parents, no inheritance, no job! I ought to make a script of my recent history to offer to a film producer to make a disaster movie. That might be the only way to make any money.

Altogether not the brightest of pictures! *Mustn't grumble though* as *they* say... the bloody fools!

I don't know how I would have got through the next few days without the support of mike who phoned me at regular intervals and Geoff who paid me a long visit. Both had the full story of my series of disasters.

Dennis Thrupp called again to say that a Chief Inspector Morgan of the police specialist team, dealing with all the recent art thefts, had called him. He had confirmed that the Orchard House case had been duly now referred to his unit and that he was in charge of the investigation. He had seemed to be very much 'on the ball', and had confirmed broadly what Jack Beale had said about the activities of the gang and how they operated. The Chief inspector was of the view that the paintings stolen from Orchard House would probably be on their way out of the country. Interpol had been alerted.

Mr. Thrupp would keep me informed as and when there was anything further to report.

There was something else, also.

'One more thing, William, I have discovered an insurance policy on your father's life of which your mother was the stated beneficiary. The insured amount is not large but at least it's something. The figure the company has given me is just over five thousand pounds. Also your mother maintained a current account at the same bank as your father and there's a credit balance of about a thousand.'

'Well, that's some consolation, better than nothing I suppose. I could really do with the money.'

'I'm afraid there's a snag.'

Well, I thought, I should have seen that coming. My whole life had become one big snag.

'What's that, then, Mr.Thrupp?'

'The local Coroner has decided to postpone the inquest to give time for your mother's body to be recovered. Of course, this is absurd– It's not as if there's any doubt about your mother's death or indeed the circumstances leading to it.'

'Well, the police told me that they would keep me informed if and when my mother was...er...found, but I've heard nothing further.'

'William, I'm sorry if this is painful for you to hear, but I took it on myself to contact the local Coastguard. They advise that, due to a combination of the outgoing tide at the relevant time and the strong off-shore currents for which that part of the coast is apparently notorious, it is more than likely that your mother's body will never be recovered. I'm told, in fact, that there have been two recent incidents at Cocklemouth involving swimmers, who were bathing off rocks near the headland, got caught in the fierce currents and were last seen struggling in the water as they were swept away. In official language, they were listed as 'missing presumed drowned' and their bodies have never been recovered.'

As I was listening to what Mr.Thrupp was saying, it struck me that, in some ways, it would be better if my mother was never found. I believe that's what she would have wished, and I could hardly bear to think of her poor bedraggled body, once so beautiful, being washed up on some lonely beach. Frankly I preferred to remember her as she was when she was alive.

'I understand, Mr.Thrupp, but perhaps Mum would have wanted it that way, the note she left virtually says so. And I must say that I've been rather dreading the inquest – the suicide note being read out in court, as presumably it would be, her extra-marital affair becoming public knowledge, the row with my father and all that, but, in any event, I don't quite see what all this has got to do with the insurance and the money at the bank.'

'Well, in these circumstances, until the inquest has taken place, the Coroner won't sign off a death certificate. Without that we can't start the process of winding up your mother's estate, as little as it is, and distributing it to you.'

'Oh, no, surely not!'

'Yes, I'm sorry, but that's sadly the case. Of course, the Coroner will no doubt have to proceed with the inquest at some point in time, whether or not your mother's body is recovered, but I can't tell you, as of now, precisely when that will be.'

'But in the meantime, I get no money – is what you're saying?'

'I'm afraid so.'

Par for the course! As *they* would doubtless say with an unsympathetic shrug of the shoulders.

✤

It was the evening before Christmas Eve, and I had spent the day tidying up my flat and washing a few shirts in preparation for my stay with Mike and his parents. I didn't feel like staying alone in the flat and besides there wasn't much left in the fridge for me to eat other than another congealed sandwich, so I thought I'd walk up the road to The White Bear, have a drink or two and go on from there for my usual curry at The Cotswold Tandoori..

When I got to the pub, it was unusually full – only natural, I suppose, being so near to Christmas. Somehow I found that the sight of so many people in a festive mood, seemingly without a care in the world, was profoundly depressing. I ought to be like them, I told myself - care-free, happy, looking forward to Christmas and a break from work, but I wasn't of course. It just wasn't fair. I nearly turned round to go back home. However, I noticed Geoff sitting in a corner by the fireplace, and I struggled through the throng of jolly revellers to reach him.

'Hello, Geoff' I said, 'What are you doing here? I thought you were off to Harrogate to spend Christmas with your parents.'

'Well, yes I should have gone today, but something came up, and I'm going tomorrow now.'

'You better catch an early train then; it's Christmas Eve tomorrow; The trains will all be full. What was this *something* that came up, then?'

Geoff looked a bit bashful.

'Well, you see, I had dinner again with Wanda last night and you know what's likely to happen when you have dinner with Wanda, don't you?! You'll understand I didn't feel like travelling today.'

'What?!

'Well you know how it is.'

'No, I don't. I can guess from what you told me, but you bloody stopped me, if you recall, from actually finding out for myself!'

'Yes, it was the noblest thing I've ever done.'

'But your noble instincts clearly failed last night! You didn't manage to stop *yourself,* did you?!'

'Look, William, let me put it like this. You know how you feel when you've had too much to drink and you wake up the next morning feeling absolutely dreadful; you vow that you're never going to touch a drop of alcohol *ever again,* not the merest sip – then the very same evening, there you are again propping up the bar...Well, I swore, after the last time, that I'd never again go near the woman and, to be fair, I didn't for months, but then I met her in the supermarket yesterday morning and...'

'I suppose it was the sight of all that Baroque splendour, as Mike would say, was it?!'

'Precisely, all that lovely, curvy, pink plumpness and...'

'Yes, no need to say any more.' I interrupted to no avail, as Geoff continued regardless.

'...and she was wearing a tight leather outfit, with lots of laces, fringes and things, and Texan-style boots. I mean, what's not to like?! She's jolly persuasive, too, you know...Won't take 'No' for an answer'

'But you knew very well what you'd be letting yourself in for...'

'Yes but, William, it would have taken a man of *iron will* to resist Wanda's invitation delivered in that deep husky voice of hers and dressed as she was, positively an *iron will*...and my will is...how shall I put it? Made of...er...rather more pliable material.'

'Well, all I can say is that you're completely depraved, worse even than Mike!'

'Yes, you're probably right. Always a sucker for a saucy smile. Anyway, how about a drink?'

'Good idea.'

The Cotswold Tandoori, across the road from the pub, was also very full and rather than eat there, we ordered some takeaways to take home to my flat. As we staggered back down the High Street, we sang 'Ding Dong Merrily on High' in an attempt to capture the Christmas spirit. Our singing might not quite have reached the high standards of the choir of Christ's College Cambridge but nobody could have faulted us for enthusiasm. Not every local inhabitant was equally appreciative of our efforts, however. A very rude man leant out of his bedroom window and told us to 'shut the fuck up!'

'Ding, dong, you miserable heathen bashtard! Don't you know it's Chrishmashtime!' Geoff shouted back at him. He would have said more along the same lines had I not managed to drag him away, and it was with some relief on my part that we finally got home to my flat without further incident.

We ate our takeaways at the kitchen table washed down with a very decent bottle of Burgundy, a premier cru Volnay, which a grateful parent of one of my former pupils had presented to me and which I had carelessly opened by mistake thinking it was something rather less special. Geoff, who enjoyed fine wines, had a fit of drunken hysterics when he realised my mistake. Worse still, Geoff drank most of it as I felt I'd had enough at the pub.

Having cleared away the debris, we talked, joked and laughed until the small hours, and for a short while I was able, if not to forget, at least to push to the back of my mind the terrible catalogue of woes that had befallen me. Finally I tumbled into bed.

Geoff had sensibly left his car at home and walked to the pub. He lived in a tiny rented cottage a good two miles away, and didn't feel in the circumstances much like walking home, so I let him sleep on my sofa.

I fell into a deep sleep almost at once.

CHAPTER TWELVE

Christmas Eve had arrived at last and I had overslept. Belatedly recalling that this was the day I was supposed to be travelling down to Exmoor, I hauled myself out of bed with a deep, prolonged sigh.

Geoff had gone, probably quite early, without waking me. He had a long journey in front of him all the way to Yorkshire. He had left, though, a note for me on the kitchen table. It read:

Dear William,

I solemnly and sincerely undertake that I shall never again touch a drop of drink or a loose woman.

Should I ever commit a breach of this undertaking, I shall, as a penance, become either a Trappist monk or a Chartered Accountant.

Wishing you a very happy Christmas,

Ding, Dong!

Geoff

What with over-sleeping and one thing and another, I was very late getting underway. After showering and packing a few things to take, I thought I ought to get something as a present for Mike's parents, so I set off for the supermarket and bought a bottle of Champagne and a box of liqueur chocolates. This all took more time than I had bargained for as, being Christmas Eve, there were of course very long queues at the checkout.

Additionally, I had left home without having had anything to eat and, feeling a bit peckish, thought I should have a light snack before embarking on my journey. I decided on a pub lunch at a place not far from the supermarket, and by the time I got there it was already nearly a quarter past one. There was a big crowd in the pub, an office party, and my food took a long time to arrive. The result of all this was that it was getting on for three o'clock before I finally reached the junction with the M5 for my journey south.

Mike had advised me to take the M5 down to the exit for the A361. After a short distance, I would find a turning off the A361 towards Bampton and Dulverton. On reaching Dulverton I was to follow the directions he had given me to Barleton Grange.

I was held up for what seemed like hours by a long tail-back of traffic leading up to the Avon Bridge where the M5 crosses over the River Avon near Bristol. The result of this and, having started out late in the first place, was that by the time I eventually reached Dulverton it was dark.

I drove through the town and took a turning to the left which I was sure would take me up to the hotel. It was one of those small West Country lanes with high hedges on both sides. After about a mile or so, the lane forked, and I took the right-hand fork on the basis that this seemed to be going upwards and Barleton Grange was, I knew, near the crest of a hill. Further on, there were other little lanes and tracks leading off to left and right. I took one of these, feeling sure, from Mike's instructions, that it was the right one, but the visibility was now extremely poor. I must have taken another couple of turnings off this lane, each time because I thought I could see a light or a building but each time it turned out to be a false trail. I was by now thoroughly lost.

The lane I found myself driving along suddenly petered out into a rough farm track. I recalled that there had been a field gate set back slightly from the track about 30 yards back, and I started to reverse hoping that there would be room for me to turn. I had only gone a few yards when the car suddenly lurched to one side. I had obviously driven into a ditch. Cursing my bad luck and by now quite panic-stricken, I put the car into first gear and tried to drive out of it. This only, however, made matters worse. The rear wheels spun and skidded on the slippery ground and, before I knew what was happening, the car skewed sideways rather than forwards causing it to slip yet further into the ditch. It was now leaning over at a most precarious angle, and a second or two later with a horrible *thwump*, it rolled over completely on its side.

With an enormous effort, I managed to push the door open and clamber out on all fours. It was bitterly cold, and there was a strong northerly wind with flurries of sleet or snow.

THIS WAS REALLY IT. THE FINAL DEFINITIVE END OF WILLIAM WILKINS! I thought as I staggered to my feet.

My life in tatters, and now I was to die from exposure in this desolate, lonely, God-forsaken place. I tried my mobile but of course there was no signal.

'God, help me, please help me!' I cried out.

Nothing but the howling wind, the swirling snow and the bitter cold. Beginning to blubber, I called out despairingly again:

'Help! For God's sake help me!'.

To my amazement, God's representative on Exmoor suddenly manifested himself in the shape of a very large man in a flat cap looming up from behind the hedge which bordered the ditch where my car had come to grief.

'That yurr car, then?' he said.

'No,' I said, out of sheer flippancy, I know not why, 'It belongs to the Queen of Sheba. I'm just guarding it for her'

'Eh?'

'Sorry. Yes, it's my car.'

'Aarh, well I don't think we can pull 'ee out tonight…Whurr you be going to, then?'

'To Barleton Grange, but I got lost…'

'Aarh, Barleton Grange eh? That be Hailey's place. Well, les' you wan' er tuck yurrself up in that thurr ditch for the night - Ah'll better be giving 'ee a ride over thurr !' He said, with what I took to be a rustic chuckle.

'That would be very kind.'

'Norra problem. Now you walk back to the iron gate – only a

few yurrds back – and I'll meet 'ee thurr.'

I collected my suitcase from the back of the car with some diffi-culty and walked the short distance to the gate where the large man in a flat cap met me. We crossed the field on foot to a stile in the hedge on the other side. The stile gave access onto another lane, where an ancient, mud-splattered Land Rover was parked. A great wave of relief surged over me.

Another ten minutes saw me safely deposited at Barleton Grange. Mike had been most concerned when I had failed to turn up, and was wondering whether to set off to scour the country lanes in search of me. Old Macdonald, or whoever he was, was invited in, and served with a pint of 'scrumpy' as a reward for my safe deliverance.

'Well, I'm glad you finally got here.' Mike's father, Malcolm, said, after I'd explained what had happened 'We were beginning to wonder where on earth you'd got to. Jolly lucky old Ted was on hand to rescue you! In fact we were just about to start dinner without you...'

'Of course, we wouldn't have started dinner without you, William' Jean, Mike's charming mother put in, casting a reproving glance at her husband, 'You poor chap – Lots of people get lost trying to find us, but most don't end up in a ditch –What a dreadful thing to happen!'

'What a prize ass!' was Mike's alternative verdict on the matter, 'You'd better go up and have a shower to warm up. I'll show you to your room.'

Having enjoyed a pleasant shower and changed into something more respectable, I felt much better as I arrived downstairs once more, though still a bit shaken by my recent experience.

'I think William needs a drink after his little adventure. Do you think we've got time for one?' Mike asked his father, and I must say I was rather pleased that he did.

'Yes, but better make it a very quick one; I'm hungry!'

Mike led me to the snug little cocktail bar, and I was surprised to find that there was a woman there on her own...not, I thought, one of the family.

'I thought you told me the hotel was closed now. Who's this lady, then?' I whispered in Mike's ear.

'Oh, she's not a hotel guest; she's a friend of my parents; lives nearby; been invited for dinner. Come on, I'll pour you a drink and then I'll introduce you.'

There was an open bottle of Champagne on the bar counter and Mike poured us both a glass, following which we went over to where the woman was sitting, near the French window. She must have been, I thought, about sixty or so, but very striking and most stylishly dressed, and she had adopted a sitting position that showed off a pair of long shapely legs to the very best advantage.

'I'd like you to meet my friend, William Wilkins' Mike said, addressing the lady, 'William, this is Mrs. Stearnley-Owen.'

'Oh, do call me Joyce, please.' She said. 'It's very nice to meet you, William.'

'And it's a pleasure to meet you too, er, Joyce.' I said.

'Well, Mike,' Joyce said, turning to face Mike, 'all your friends seem quite charming and William is no exception, but underneath that innocent exterior, I'm sure he's just as much a rogue as you are; he must be if he's a friend of yours!'

Mike laughed.

'Don't pay any attention to Joyce, William. She thinks all men are rogues!'

'Of course they are, most of them, but the truth is I can forgive them everything provided they're charming and funny. Of course, your dear father, Mike, is an exception; he manages to be both charming, witty and a perfect gentleman without the slightest hint of roguery...My late husband wasn't a rogue either but he was a terrible old bore; I could pardon him for that, though, because he was terribly rich, died early and left me all his money...'

I was about to plead that I was quite as innocent as I looked, but regrettably had no money, when Malcolm put his head round the door.

'Come on you lot; dinner's ready.'

'Joyce is quite a card, isn't she?!' Mike whispered to me as we trooped into the dining room. I'll tell you all about her later.'

CHAPTER THIRTEEN

Barleton Grange was not one of those smart boutique hotels which receive glowing accolades in the travel supplements of the Sunday newspapers. Instead, it had a cosy, homely feel to it...appropriately enough as it was not simply a hotel, but also, of course, home to Mike's family.

The dining room normally accommodated six separate tables for hotel guests, but for the Christmas period, these had been removed and replaced by one large circular table. There was of course that 'de rigueur' requirement for cosiness – a log fire duly 'roaring' and both room and table were garlanded with appropriately festive decorations. It all looked, indeed, very Christmassy.

The assembled company comprised Mike and I, his parents Malcolm and Jean, his sister Sarah and her husband Sam, Joyce Stearnley-Owen, a kindly old gentleman living on his own in Dulverton, whom Mike parents had also thoughtfully invited, and the latter's elderly black Labrador. I didn't catch the old boy's name but the dog's name, Mike told me, was Puke – but that was almost certainly Mike's idea of a joke, it was probably Duke.

The food was quite delicious, all cooked by Mike's mother as the regular hotel chef was taking his Christmas break. I must say it was a very convivial occasion and, like my recent evening with Geoff, helped distract me from my troubles.

Mike, Joyce and Malcolm kept up a lively banter all evening, keeping the rest of us entertained and amused.

The old gentleman fell asleep from time to time and his dog also slumbered as he lay stretched out by the fire; both snored and dribbled, but, in a seasonal spirit of goodwill, we all pretended not to notice.

After dinner, Joyce, the old gent and his dog departed. Despite offers of help, Jean insisted that the clearing up be left until the morning and both she and Malcolm went off to bed, as did Mike's sister and her husband.

Mike suggested a final nightcap and the two of us repaired once more to the bar.

'You were going to tell me more about Joyce' I said, 'I'm dying to hear!'

'Quite right, I was, she's fantastic, isn't she? I think she's one of the sexiest women I've ever met. I get the hots on every time I see her.'

'Well, I can see that Joyce is a very well-preserved lady and all that and quite striking, but, she's old enough to be your mother.'

'So, what?! She's gorgeous!'

'Oh, really Mike! Why are you salivating over Joyce's charms, when you've got the lovely young Tina to go out with?'

'Not any more, I'm afraid. Tina and I have split up – not that we were really ever an item. Tina's just a tease – there was never anything serious between us...and all those rumours about her seducing half the Junior Common Room – just a load of tosh!'

'Well, I'm sorry, about you and Tina, I mean.'

'Yes, so am I, nice girl, but there it is. We're still good friends.'

'You were telling me about Joyce' I said, after a tactful pause.

'Yes, I was, wasn't I?' Mike continued, getting himself back up to speed. 'Well, Joyce, Joyce Owen as she was born, is the daughter of a Cardiff solicitor. After school, she studied Drama at University with a view to a career in the theatre, but she never finished her degree. Instead, she became a fashion model working for an agency in London. She's gorgeous now but she must have been an absolute sensation when she was a young model.'

A bit like my mother, I thought, a thought tinged by a moment of sadness.

'Well' Mike continued, 'It wasn't long before she began to move in quite elevated circles, and managed to hook a filthy rich banker called Julian Stearnley, a man well-connected in all the right places.

After a short engagement, they were married –quite the talk of the town, I gather.

'Well, poor Stearnley was old enough to be her father, if not her grandfather, and not in the best of health. About five years later, he suffered a stroke, while lunching at his club, and snuffed it, leaving Joyce an enormous fortune. Within a month or two of the funeral, she had bought herself a large house in one of the most fashionable parts of north London.

'She could, no doubt, have afforded to live a life of a luxury without lifting a finger, but she had other ambitions and set about establishing a business to run from her newly acquired mansion ...'

'What type of business?' I asked.

'An exclusive private members' club. It was a great success, too. Joyce ran it for a long time until she finally packed it in about three years ago, sold the house to a Saudi businessman and moved down here for a well-earned retirement. She no doubt made another stupendous fortune from the sale of the house to add to the one she'd already inherited, not to mention all the money she must have made out of the club business.'

'But, what sort of club was it – I mean what did they do there?'

'Well, my parents, to this day, believe it was a private dining club where the 'Great and Good' met to discuss the affairs of the nation and other weighty matters...'

'Well, what was it, then?' I asked again, intrigued.

'It was a club where posh chaps went to be spanked, caned, walloped and otherwise humiliated at enormous expense.'

'No? I don't believe it!'

'Oh, yes – Spanking, 'le Vice Anglais', remains very popular, you know, in the higher reaches of the metropolitan classes and the business world. If you've ever read the tabloids, you'd know that Joyce's club was hardly the first of its type by a long chalk nor will it be the last. It did have a certain special cachet, though, and guaranteed complete discretion. The members included the usual coterie of eminent lawyers, politicians, senior civil servants, military figures, a brace of Bishops – *High Church* of course – hedge fund managers, brokers and other city types along with a smattering of super-rich businessmen.'

'Good God!'

'Joyce, you'll have gathered, is a *dominatrix*.'

'But how do you come to know about all this? Presumably, Joyce didn't tell you herself?'

'No, though she drops the odd hint occasionally. It was actually an old school friend of mine, Ben Haskins, who told me the full story. Ben works as a commodity broker in the City and, one Friday evening, his boss took him along to the club as his guest as a special treat.

'While Madam Joyce was administering a blistering caning to Ben's boss in the library, Ben himself was led to a room upstairs, where two strapping Bulgarian girls held him down while a tall, wiry Russian woman in a thong thrashed his backside mercilessly with a thick leather strap. When the Russian lady had quite finished with him, he had sex with the one of the Bulgarian girls while the other one gently rubbed some soothing balm into his throbbing posterior.

'Afterwards, it was pink Champagne and chocolate truffles all round – What a great start to the weekend, don't you think?!'

'Extraordinary!'

'Though Joyce is now officially retired as a dominatrix...'

'You mean as oppose to continuing to work in an *official* capacity as a dominatrix?!'

'Oh, Ha, Ha. Don't be silly, William! You know what I mean. What I was going to say is that she still performs certain favours for some of her old clients.'

'How do you know?'

'Well, Ben told me his boss comes to see her from time to time and there are others I'm sure. Look, William, why don't we pay Joyce a visit. She thinks we're both very naughty boys and you know what happens to naughty boys!'

'You're not serious, surely?'

'Well, why not? It would be fun – a great new experience!'

'No, no, no. Absolutely not!'

'Oh, you are an old bore, William.'

'Better bore than sore!' I replied, rather pithily. 'And, now I think it's time I went to bed.'

CHAPTER FOURTEEN

Christmas day dawned bright and cold. There'd even been a sprinkling of snow during the night and the hotel gardens, of which I had a good view from my bedroom window, shone in the morning sun with a sparkling beauty adding a new lustre to their natural prettiness – a perfect Christmas morning.

In many ways, too, it was the best of Christmas days – Church, carols, warm fires, and chilled Champagne...not to mention another lavish dinner served with exquisite wines from Malcolm's cellar.

For me, though, it was a difficult day for obvious reasons. A day of happiness and sadness combined – Happy and grateful to be where I was; sad not to be where I ought to have been if fate had not so cruelly intervened.

I missed my parents most terribly on this of all days, and none of the facile expressions, which those anonymous *they* might offer to console me, could hope to assuage the sense of loss and pain which I felt.

Despite all the kindness shown to me that Christmas day, I was relieved when it was over, and I could retire alone to bed and find the welcome oblivion of sleep.

CHAPTER FIFTEEN

'I thought we should go for a nice brisk walk down to Tarr Steps after breakfast.' Mike said, next morning, 'It's a beautiful day and Boxing Day is, after all, a good day for a reviving walk in the countryside.'

Breakfast was quite a feast. Mike's mother had excelled herself: wonderful crispy bacon, properly made local sausages, lovely poached eggs, sauté potatoes, splendid squashy tomatoes and of course black pudding. Gently breaking wind, as I left the table, I walked over to the window and looked out. Mike was right. It was indeed a beautiful morning with the sun shining out of a clear cloudless sky. Rolling countryside stretched away on all sides under a pristine blanket of snow. There had obviously been another fall, heavier this time, during night as evidenced by the depth of snow on the roofs of nearby cottages.

I was, though, I confess, a little dubious about the proposed walk. Would this turn out to be another of Mike's 'adventures' more like an Arctic expedition than a gentle stroll in the English countryside? I asked myself.

I had never been there, but understood that Tarr Steps was an interesting example of an ancient clapper bridge in a beautiful setting in the valley of the River Barle. No doubt it would be all the better for the absence of day-trippers flocking there in the summer months, but was this quite the day to walk there? The countryside looked very pretty enough with all that virgin snow shimmering in the sunlight but surely it was best viewed safely through the window of the residents' lounge.

'Mike, I haven't got any suitable boots for walking in the snow.' I said, believing that I had found the perfect excuse to sit in comfort by the fire and read a book. No such luck!

'No problem. I've several spare pairs and we have the same size feet, remember.'

'Well, oughtn't I go and see about my car?' That's got him, I thought.

'Old Ted Fowler – he's the one who rescued you on Christmas Eve, in case you didn't catch the name – is sorting all that out for you. Ted's knows some bloke over at Barle Cross who runs the local garage and he's promised to get the car towed over there tomorrow. Ted owes us a favour or two. Dad owns the field on the other side of the lane opposite here and lets him graze his sheep there for practically nothing.'

'Well, it's very kind of Ted to take all that trouble'.

There was nothing for it. I had no option now but to accompany Mike on his beastly walk. Tarr Steps was a little distance away, and Mike had originally suggested that we should walk the whole way. I put my foot down on this one and Mike grudgingly agreed that we would drive at least part of the way there.

I wondered whether the roads would be passable after the night before, but Mike proposed that he borrow his father's Land Rover. He was completely confident that this elderly vehicle, an even more dilapidated specimen than that belonging to the estimable Mr. Fowler, could negotiate almost anything in any weather, and the walk through the deep snow would be a challenge, a test for my lazy soul. It would apparently, as Mike put it, rejuvenate my spirit by reconnecting me with my pre-historic roots as a hunter-gatherer or some such idiocy. In essence, he told me that it would be 'good for me'. Every time I hear that dread phrase, whether applied to some sugar free, fibre-rich form of nourishment which I am invited to sample, or some healthy, life-enhancing activity in which it is recommended that I should indulge, I know instinctively that I am not going to like it. Mike's walk, I felt sure, would be such a case.

The side roads were still pretty appalling, and the untreated main road was not a great deal better. More than once we nearly skidded off the carriageway. Several times I suggested that we should turn back but Mike would have none of it. It seemed to take an eternity to get to the place that Mike had selected as the starting point for our walk, but at last we arrived. We put on our boots and set forth to tramp through the powdery snow. Not surprisingly, nobody else was about, and there was an all-pervasive silence and blissful aura of peace about the country that morning. May be it was worth it after all, I thought to myself, though, of course, I refrained from admitting as much to Mike.

Without talking much, we trudged on through the snow downwards into the valley of the Barle. At last we reached Tarr Steps, and I must say that I was quite overwhelmed by the beauty of the scene. The bridge itself was covered in deep snow, and each of the boulders and rocks large enough to protrude above the surface of the icy waters had its own snowy crest. The trees marched up the steep hillsides on either side of the river like soldiers in some fairy-tale army, resplendent in their glittering white uniforms. A thin gossamery mist hovered over the water.

I nearly said something to Mike about this stunning sight, but managed to stop myself in time. It would only encourage him to dream up some new adventure, I feared, involving a long, and quite probably dangerous, romp to some other remote area of the moor.

'Quite pretty, eh?' Mike said, eventually breaking the silence.

'Yes,' I agreed 'quite pretty'.

Then we trudged back up the hill and across the moor to where the battered Land Rover was parked.

CHAPTER SIXTEEN

The next day, the wind changed direction. A warm blustery wind, accompanied by squally showers, blew in from the Bristol Channel causing a fast thaw. By the end of the day, all the snow had more or less disappeared. Gushing rivulets of water from the melting snow poured off the hills swelling the rivers and streams.

The few days left of my stay passed quickly. The fields and woodland paths had become damp and muddy, and, happily, that ruled out all but the shortest of walks. Instead we made excursions in Mike's car, generally finishing up for a snack lunch at a country pub in a pretty hamlet or nestling remotely in a deep wooded combe...and at the end of the day, there was always a magnificent dinner to look forward to.

On the return from one such excursion, Mike's father informed me that the garage had phoned to say my car was ready. Apparently, the damage was not as bad as originally thought. One of the wheels had had to be replaced along with the exhaust and the rear windscreen. Otherwise, the damage was largely superficial – a lot of minor dents and scratches...adding to the many dents and scratches already there.

I'd made up my mind, albeit reluctantly, that once the car was ready, I ought to return home.

All good things as *they*, those dreary folk, would probably proclaim *must come to an end.*

CHAPTER SEVENTEEN

At breakfast the next day, the 30 of December, Mike kindly offered to drive me over to the garage to collect the car.

'I'll take you over there after lunch' He said, 'Can't go this morning, I'm afraid, got to help Dad re-erect part of the garden face which blew down in the wind the other day.'

'Tell you what, though, William. It's a lovely morning – why don't you take a walk over to Witt's Wood and back? You take the bridleway at the back of here for about a mile and a half until you come to a Forestry Commission sign. The bridleway then meets a rough track; one way leads through the wood, but you take the track in the other direction which soon becomes a tarmac drive and in about a half a mile or so, you'll come to the road to Dulverton; when you get to the road, turn left and that will bring you in about another mile straight back up here to the house.

'There're some good open views towards the moor along the way and some attractive cottages and farmhouses. You'll enjoy it, and you don't even need walking boots.'

I'm always naturally suspicious of Mike's suggestions, but this seemed not too demanding an enterprise, and after breakfast I duly set off.

Mike was right; there were some outstanding moorland views from the bridleway, and, along the lane leading to the Dulverton road, there were indeed some pretty thatched cottages and an old Exmoor 'longhouse', the traditional type of moorland farm, evocatively dominating the brow of a hill.

Further down the lane, not far from the Dulverton Road, I came upon a substantial stone farmhouse, not another longhouse this time, but altogether a rather grander property. It was called 'Witt's Manor Farm' and was set back a little from the lane, surrounded by well tended gardens. The house itself, early Georgian by the look of it, was quite imposing and had obviously been given a gentrifying makeover fairly recently. I guessed that it was no longer used as a farm but was now an up-market home for some townie with loads of cash to spare.

As I passed the garden gate, I heard a barking voice which I immediately recognised. It was, without a doubt, the voice of Sir Giles Pendleton, the Chairman of Governors of Hanfield Manor School. I turned round to look, ducking to conceal myself behind a convenient hedge. Sure enough, there in the doorway stood Sir Giles' portly figure and clearly visible, just behind him, presumably the owner of Witt's Manor Farm, Madam Spanker herself, Joyce Stearnley-Owen.

'I hope you liked my new cane. Giles' Joyce said, 'It's got a nice easy swing and gives a good sharp sting, doesn't it? A sting in the tail, I suppose you might say!'

'Oh, rather' Sir Giles barked, 'I can still feel it now!'

'Well, you know what I always say, Giles – the greater the pain, the greater the pleasure to follow!'

'Absolutely!'

'Look, Giles, I'm sorry I can't ask you to stay on for a bit longer, but I've a lot to do this morning. You see, I've got the Vicar coming to lunch.'

After a final fond embrace, Sir Giles walked slowly and rather stiffly the short distance down the front path to the garden gate. His car was parked in the road just outside, and I had hoped that he wouldn't see me lurking by the hedge, but he did.

'Ah, Wilson. What are you doing here?'

'It's Wilkins, Sir, actually, I've been staying over Christmas with Mike Hailey and his family.

'Mike Hailey?'

'Mike teaches Physics at Hanfield, Sir.'

'Ah, yes, yes, of course. Now, Wilson... *kins*, I mean... I should be most grateful if you wouldn't say anything... er, er... about my being here today. My visit concerned a matter erm, of the upmost delicacy, but it's vital, quite vital, that it should remain confidential, do you understand?'

'Of course, I quite understand, sir; you may rely on my complete discretion.'

'Good, good. Well, must be off now – Governors' meeting this evening and all that. Good day to you, then, Wilson. See you next term.'

I didn't disabuse him of his belief that he would be seeing me – or for that matter poor John Wilson – next term, but simply watched as he lowered himself very gingerly into the driver's seat of his car, turned the car round and drove away, managing, I observed with some satisfaction, to scrape his off-side front wing on the wall of a neighbouring cottage as he disappeared at some speed up the road.

When Sir Giles had gone, I set off again, walking with renewed energy in my stride. I could hardly wait to get back and tell Mike what I'd just seen and heard.

Mike was quite ecstatic when I reported what had occurred, and almost choked with laughter. He insisted on a glass of Champagne before lunch.

'I give you a toast.' he said, 'To the Chairman's fat arse, long way it sting!'

'Long may it sting!' I echoed, with feeling.

Despite protestations from Mike and his family who had invited me to stay on to see the New Year in, I remained firm in my resolve to return home after picking up the car from the garage. I badly needed to get on with completing my CV and sending off job applications.

Mike drove me over to there and very kindly paid the bill for the repairs. I could pay him back, he said, when I'd got myself a new job. He made one last attempt to persuade me to stay.

'Look, William' he said, 'in this brave new digital world, you don't need to be at home or anywhere in particular to do whatever needs doing. The hotel is closed till the 5th of January. Why not stay on?'

I knew, though, that there'd be too many distractions at Barleton Grange, and besides, I thought that it was time for me to go. I didn't want to abuse the hospitality of Mike's parents by over-staying my welcome.

So I set out for home, not without regret as I had greatly enjoyed my stay and Mike's persuasive manner had nearly caused me to change my mind.

As it turned out, it was well that I returned home when I did, and not purely for the reasons I had in mind at the time.

CHAPTER EIGHTEEN

My father had many friends and acquaintances, many of whom were in some way connected with the art world and most of whom I had never met. I had, however, met his old friend, Godfrey Bull, on several occasions over the years. Godfrey lived in Bath where they had first become acquainted during the time when Dad had a gallery there, before his move to Cheltenham.

Godfrey and my father shared an interest in old Delftware, both of Dutch and English origin. In my father's case, this obviously took second place to his interest in fine art, but he had nevertheless assembled, over the years, a modest collection of plates, jugs, vases and so forth including some quite rare and valuable pieces – all now regrettably stolen. In Godfrey's case, however, collecting Delft was an abiding passion, if not an obsession.

Although he possessed some fine examples of early English Delftware made in Bristol and Liverpool, the pride of Godfrey's collection tended to be classic blue and white examples of seventeenth-century Royal Delft made in Delft itself, and perhaps his interest in old Delftware may have arisen, partly at least, because of his Dutch connections. His mother was Dutch and had met his father while she was working at the Dutch consulate in London. She had sadly passed away some years ago but Godfrey remained in regular touch with his aunt, Fleur, his mother's younger sister.

Fleur lived with her husband, Hendrik, in a beautiful apartment on the second floor of an old step-gabled house in the Bloemgracht in Amsterdam to which Godfrey was a frequent visitor. Indeed, on the day before I drove down to Exmoor to stay with Mike and his family, Godfrey had flown to Amsterdam to spend Christmas and the New Year with Fleur and Hendrik, though of course I knew nothing of any of this.

Like his father before him, Godfrey had spent his working life as an optician with a chain of shops in the Bath and Bristol area, operating under the catchy trade name 'Bull's Eye Care'. He had been retired, though, for several years, having sold out the business on quite profitable terms to one of the large national chains.

On a crisp, clear day between Christmas and the New Year, Godfrey's aunt and her husband were off to the nearby city of Haarlem to visit friends, so he had some time to himself. Many folk, in such circumstances, might dawdle over a late breakfast in their dressing gowns and waste much of the day, but not Godfrey.

Godfrey had always been a very methodical man. There was method in everything he did, including the way in which he thought it appropriate to dress for any particular task or occasion. He needed, he thought, on this day to wear something in which he would feel comfortable doing the things he planned to do, not only during the course of the day but also something which would be suitable for the evening as he would not be returning to the flat before bedtime. He always liked to appear smart and while his taste in clothes was conventional, indeed old fashioned, he liked to add a little touch of flamboyance. Thus, he chose, after much thought, his Donegal tweed suit and a rather racy red bow tie with yellow spots. As the day, though bright, was quite chilly, he would take his camel overcoat and wear the silk paisley-patterned scarf which had belonged to his late father and the rakish brown trilby that his father used to wear to Saturday race meetings.

Thus suitably attired, he sallied forth early with a spring in his step and a happy feeling of joie de vivre. In addition to collecting Delftware, Godfrey had three other great passions in life. As a bachelor, denied the pleasures and responsibilities of marriage and fatherhood, he perhaps needed these things to give a meaning and shape to his life, and he owed his cheerful mood that day to the fact that he planned to indulge each and every one of his four great passions before bedtime. Of course, he had conceived of a carefully worked out plan of action to enable him to achieve this ambitious objective.

His first port of call, which involved only a short walk, was his favourite cafe, a charming old place founded in the seventeenth century, at the junction of the Prinsengracht canal with the Brouwersgracht. Here, he would indulge the first on the list of his great passions – a giant piece of Appelgebak, Dutch apple pie, with a great dollop of whipped cream. He ordered a strong coffee too, of course, and was unable to resist a second piece of Appelgebak. This, it was true, involved a slight deviation from his plan but he thought it fully justified as it would keep him going, without the need for lunch, until the evening when he had booked a restaurant for an early supper.

The second destination on his itinerary was an antique shop in the Spiegelgracht, an area renowned for antique shops, and the particular shop he intended to visit specialised in old Delftware, the greatest of his passions. To reach the Spiegelgracht involved quite a long walk and Godfrey had decided that he would cross over the Prinsengracht and the Keizergracht to the lovely Herengracht, the innermost of the three canals making up what is called the Canal Ring. As the weather was fine and sunny, he would make the most of it, strolling at a relaxed pace and enjoying the fine views of the canal, its bridges and the beautiful canal-side buildings.

The proprietor of the shop he was to visit, Lotte Van De Groot, was a delightful woman, and Godfrey had patronised her shop for many years. Indeed, he had purchased there many fine pieces of Delftware which together comprised a not insignificant part of his collection. In fact, on every visit to Amsterdam, he made a point of visiting the shop. It was one of those places in which it was simply a pleasure to browse, but he nearly always bought something, and this time was no exception.

Godfrey derived great pleasure, too, from his conversations with Lotte with whom, as a valued customer he was on personal name terms. Lotte was a respected authority on old Delftware and a most charming person, but these were not the only attributes which attracted Godfrey's admiration. Lotte also happened to be a singularly attractive lady with a curvaceous figure and an ample bosom...which brings us to the third of Godfrey's great passions, not one to which he openly admitted, but a passion nevertheless; the fact is that Godfrey was obsessed with Breasts, *Big* Breasts... Lotte's breasts would certainly meet the desired criteria, but, despite his purchase of a delightful early-nineteenth-century sauce boat at quite a salty price, Godfrey could hardly ask her to bare her bosom for his inspection, could he? He had other plans, though.

Having spent a long time at the shop happily browsing and chatting with Lotte, he really needed to move on, but as he picked up the package containing the little sauce boat and prepared to leave, he noticed out of the corner of his eye a glass display cabinet at the back of the shop which somehow he'd missed. Out of curiosity, he went over to take a look.

The cabinet contained a pair of seventeenth-century blue and white Royal Delft mantle vases of a slightly unusual design. He felt certain that he had seen these before and he knew where: they used to stand, he believed, on the mantelpiece in the drawing room at Orchard House in Cheltenham, the home of his old friend, Theo Wilkins. He knew, of course, that Theo had recently passed away and, through a mutual friend, he had also learnt with sorrow about the subsequent tragic death of Marcia Wilkins and of the burglary from Orchard House. His belief was that the vases in the display cabinet were stolen property, and he felt he had no alternative but to take the matter up with Lotte and he duly did so there and then.

'Oh, *Nee*!' Lotte had said. He must be mistaken. She had bought the vases from a most respectable Italian gentleman along with a whole collection of jugs, bowls, plates and ornaments. Only the vases were currently on display; the rest of the collection was still boxed up in her store room. They were all seventeenth- or eighteenth-century pieces of the highest quality. He had told Lotte that he was a banker who had worked for years for a bank in Amsterdam, and had presented her with a business card printed with the name of the bank and his own name 'Carlo Brighella,

Associate Manager'. He was, he told her, returning to Italy quite shortly to take up an appointment as manager of the branch of the bank in Milan. There was no space in his new apartment in Italy for his collection of Delftware and with great regret –there was actually a tear in his eye – he had decided to sell. A colleague had given him Lotte's name.

Lotte had agreed to purchase the entire collection for a substantial sum. At Sgr Brighella's request, Lotte had arranged for payment in cash because he had no wish to declare the transaction to the Italian revenue authorities.

Well, there it was, thought Godfrey, he must have been wrong after all. Wishing Lotte a fond *Vaarwel* in his best Dutch, he set off once more.

This time he was headed for 'de Walletjes', the oldest quarter of Amsterdam. It was not, however, out of any historical interest that he intended going there, but because the area was home to the Red Light District. For some years past, he had visited the same establishment in that famous, or rather infamous, district because he had taken a fancy to a particular girl there, half Dutch half Estonian, whose name was Anna and whose breasts were every man's dream. She had a cracking pair of legs, too, and Godfrey had come to realise that he liked legs almost as much as he liked breasts.

It would clearly be in poor taste to dwell on Godfrey's private moments with Anna, but as he walked away towards Dam Square, his face was a little flushed and his bow tie was certainly in need of some adjustment to restore the desired butterfly look. There was, though, a new perkiness to his stride and he wore his trilby hat tilted at even jauntier angle than his father had done after a successful day at the races.

On reaching Dam Square, he decided to stop at a bar for a refreshing beer and after whiling away some time there he took a taxi to the restaurant where he was due to meet Aunt Fleur and Hendrik on their return from Haarlem. The restaurant was close to the Conncertgebouw, Amsterdam's great concert hall, and he had reserved a table for an early supper because he had bought tickets for all three of them to attend a concert at the Concertgebouw that evening. Godfrey's fourth passion was the music of Mozart and the programme for the concert happily included a performance of Mozart's great D minor piano concerto, his particular favourite.

It had altogether been a most rewarding day. Godfrey had achieved everything he set out to do, but as he sat listening to Mozart's sublime music, his thoughts kept returning to that pair of vases at Lotte's shop. He remained convinced, despite the evidence to the contrary, that they were indeed stolen property.

The next day, he returned to Lotte's shop and asked to see the rest of the collection. Lotte took him to the store room and his inspection of all the other pieces together left him in no doubt – The whole collection, including the vases, belonged, without any question in his mind, to his old, sadly departed friend, Theo Wilkins.

CHAPTER NINETEEN

As soon as I entered my flat that evening on my return from Exmoor, the happier mood that had taken hold during my stay with Mike and his family rapidly began to evaporate.

The place was freezing cold, having been left unheated for nearly a week, and looked generally miserable and uninviting. Patches of penetrating damp had begun to appear by the bedroom window and round the sky-light in the hallway. It was altogether a depressing scene.

I turned the heating on, but it would take some time to warm up, and shivering slightly, I put on a thick jumper.

I was in the middle of unpacking my suitcase with the few things I'd taken to Exmoor with me when the phone rang.

With some hesitation, I picked up the phone. It was my father's old friend from Bath and fellow collector of Delftware, Godfrey Bull, except he wasn't phoning from Bath but from Amsterdam. He had managed to get hold of my number through Jack Beale at The Orchard Gallery. There was a note of excitement in his voice.

'William, Good news!' he said. 'I've found all your father's Delftware at an antique shop here in Amsterdam.'

Mr. Bull then proceeded to give me a full account of the circumstances in which the discovery had come about. The Dutch police had been summoned, he told me, and had, that morning, impounded the entire collection pending further enquiries. They would be notifying their British counterparts. The culprit, who had sold the stolen Delftware to the shop, was apparently an Italian, going by the name of Carlo Brighella, purporting to be the associate manager of a Dutch bank. He seemed most respectable and had presented the shop owner with a personalised business card which seemed totally authentic but which was obviously a fake. The police said that it was likely that a European arrest warrant would shortly be issued. Quite possibly, Mr. Bull suggested, the arrest of this person might lead also to the apprehension of the rest of the criminal gang and the recovery of my father's art collection.

'Marvellous!' I said. 'Wonderful news And, Mr. Bull, may I thank you so much for letting me know and for everything you've done.'

Well, well, I thought, some really good news for once! At last, perhaps, a reason to be hopeful!

I thought I ought to advise Mr. Thrupp immediately of this promising development. His office was now closed, but a bit later I was able to speak to him on the phone at his home.

He sounded at first as encouraged as I was before reverting to cautious lawyer mode.

'Look, William, you mustn't raise your hopes too much. 'Brighella' is most likely a false name and this fellow will probably be very difficult to trace, let alone the rest of the gang or indeed any of the stolen paintings.'

'Yes, I suppose you're right.' I said, coming down to earth with a bump.

'But at least the Delftware's been recovered, William, and the collection must be worth a tidy sum. It's a good start.'

As I set out that evening to collect a takeaway from the Cotswold Tandoori, I was in a pensive mood. Was the discovery of the Delftware as much of a step forward as I'd hoped? Well, in one sense, it certainly was, the collection would certainly be worth quite a lot of money, though when I would actually get anything wasn't clear. I feared there could be a lengthy delay. I agreed with Mr. Thrupp's view that this crook Brighella would probably be difficult to find, but at least there was some sort of lead. I could but hope for the best.

CHAPTER TWENTY

I got up early the next day, New Year's Eve, determined to make some progress with completing my CV and compiling a list of schools to send it to. I'd just started to tinker with the CV when I got a call on my mobile.

'Hi, William'

'Hello' I said. The caller was female, sounded young, but I didn't recognise the voice.

'It's Tina here; Mike gave me your number.'

'Tina!'

'Well, don't sound so shocked, William!'

'I'm not shocked, just surprised –pleasantly surprised.'

'Well, that's good! Look, I just called to see if you'd like to come over to my place this evening for a few drinks and a bite to eat to see the New Year in.'

'Oh, Tina, that would be great. Thank you very much; I'd love to.'

'See you this evening, then. Do you know where I live?'

Having given me her address and some brief directions, she rang off with a cheery good-bye.

Well, that's good! I thought, as I got up from my chair to go to the kitchen to make myself a cup of coffee before resuming work on the CV. I'd had frankly no idea what I was going to do that evening – probably nothing but spend a miserable evening alone in my flat – and Tina's invitation gave me something to look forward to.

Tina rented a flat above a shop in Stroud which she shared with another girl. I found it without difficulty and was able to park the car nearby quite easily. It was only just on eight when I arrived.

As I rang the entry phone bell, I wondered who else would be there: probably some friends of Tina whom I'd be unlikely to know, but perhaps there might one or two of the younger teachers or staff from the school for me to talk to.

A moment later, I heard the sound of Tina's voice through the crackly intercom: 'Come straight up'. I climbed the steep stairs to the landing where she was waiting to greet me.

Her flatmate was apparently away, staying with her parents in London, and, as I entered the flat, I looked round but there didn't seem to be any one else there.

'Am I the first to arrive, then?' I asked, 'Sorry if I'm a bit early.'

'Oh, there's no-one else coming. It's just you and me.'

'Oh!'

Wanda's 'just the two of us' invitation before Christmas sprang to mind. Don't be a fool, I told myself, it won't be like that. But I found myself, nevertheless, not quite able to dismiss the thought, vain hope that it might be. Tina after all was a very pretty girl.

'Well, there's no-one else much around. I didn't want to spend the evening on my own or go to a rowdy pub, and I thought you might like a bit of company. Mike's told me what a dreadful time you've been having.' She said, handing me a glass of Champagne.

'I must say it's very kind of you, Tina, to ask me. Incidentally, I'm sorry to hear about you and Mike splitting up.'

'Oh, don't be – Mike and I were never really together in the first place so we couldn't really split up, could we?'

'I suppose not. In fact, Mike said much the same thing, but I think he was sorry all the same.'

'Well, we're still very good friends. I like him a lot'

'That's good. I'm pleased to hear it.'

'Oh, and William, another thing you ought to know – I haven't had lots of affairs or flings or whatever you might have heard people say about me – In fact there's been nothing like that with anyone at all. I may like to flirt a bit, I admit, but that's as far as it goes.'

'I've no doubt about that, but a charming girl like you must surely have some nice boyfriend in tow.'

'Well, I don't actually at present, but I do have someone in mind if I can get him interested.'

'Really! –Who's this lucky bloke then? Or perhaps I shouldn't ask? Sorry, very rude of me.'

'Oh, I don't mind – Have a guess!'

I went through a list of the younger teachers at Hanfield, but she shook her head.

'Try again.'

'Oh, my God – it's not Geoff, is it?'

'Of course not! Anyway, he's been seeing someone else.'

'Really?' I said as innocently as I could.

'Oh, come on, William, you know perfectly well what I'm talking about and who it is too!'

'I was sworn to secrecy.'

'Well everyone in the school office knows, even the tea lady. Wanda's not terribly discreet, you know.'

'If it's not Geoff then, who is this heart throb of yours?'

'It's you, William, you silly! Why do you think you're here?'

'What me?! But, but... we've hardly ever spoken to each other before this evening.'

'I know. Mike said that you are a bit of a shrinking violet, rather shy in the company of girls.'

'Did he indeed?!'

'My brother Simon once said that the best thing to do with shrinking violets is to fertilize them with Champagne. Your glass is empty, by the way; let me fill it up for you.'

'Thanks.'

'You see. I think you're really good-looking, the best looking of all the teachers at Hanfield, in fact.'

'Really?' I said, blushing pinker than the *Financial Times*.

'And I think you find me attractive, too, because I caught you looking at me once in the same way as the sixth form boys do.'

It was quite true, I had to admit to myself, blushing all the more.

'But you never tried to chat me up, though,' Tina continued 'so I thought I'd give it a go myself and see what happened... Now, I've made you all embarrassed. A bit more fertilizer required, I think. Let me top you up again.'

This was not the light buffet supper that I imagined it would be. Tina had prepared a wonderful feast –a beef casserole followed by a crumble with winter fruits. Her brother Simon's splendid advice with regard to shrinking violets had proved undoubtedly accurate and my earlier embarrassment quickly evaporated. We opened another bottle of Champagne, which I'd brought with me, just in case the violet suffered any renewed shrinkage but this was hardly likely. In fact, we got on famously as if we had been good friends for years.

I'm not sure it's quite true to say that we 'saw in the New Year' together, except in the sense that neither of us had obviously retired for the night. We had not counted down the seconds to mid-night nor linked arms to sing Auld Lang Syne. In fact, by the time we had quite finished eating and drinking and I looked at my watch, it was already twelve-thirty.

'Good Lord, it's the New Year already!'

'Well, I hope it'll be lot better one for you than the last one.' Tina replied, leaning over to give me a kiss.

'I certainly hope so...and I can't thank you enough for everything, Tina. It's been a wonderful evening. I've really enjoyed myself...and, perhaps, we might get to see a bit more of each other, I mean if you'd like to.'

'Of course, I would!'

'Look, Tina, I'm a bit embarrassed to ask, but I think I've had a bit too much to drink, rather over-fertilized, as it were, and I don't think I really ought to drive home. Would you mind awfully if I slept on your sofa tonight?'

'Yes, I would mind, but you can come to bed with me if you like.' She said with a lovely smile.

So I did.

CHAPTER TWENTY-ONE

I must have been about thirteen years old when my parents took me to Paris for the first time. My father had been invited to attend an art exhibition at a gallery in the seventh arrondissement, and we stayed nearby at a stylish hotel, called 'Hotel Camélia', in the Rue de Rapp. It was a beautiful early nineteenth century building which, like several other buildings in the Rue de Rapp, was designed in the art nouveau style.

The internal areas of the hotel were quite as lovely as the exterior and most of the original decorative features in the entrance hall and public rooms had been preserved. It was the original lift, though, that was especially fascinating. It had wonderful decorative iron gates, a mahogany-panelled interior with inlays of classic art nouveau tulip motifs and, on its ceiling, characteristic of the style and period, a gorgeous, coloured glass, flush ceiling light.

There was even a lift attendant, a charming old boy called Anwar who came originally from French Somaliland. He wore a splendid blue uniform trimmed with gold braid. At the time of our visit, let alone now, there could surely not have been too many lifts of that vintage still in use and even fewer, if any, operated by a lift attendant – and a liveried one at that – but then the Hotel Camélia was a glorious anachronism belonging to an age of elegance long past. That, of course, was precisely what appealed to its regular guests of which Dad was certainly of the number; he simply adored the place.

The wonderful old lift was not, one has to say, an ideal form of conveyance for people in a hurry. When Anwar pressed the relevant button, nothing happened for several seconds. There was then a funny whirring noise and, after another pause, one felt the lift give a slight quiver. There followed yet a further lengthy interval, during which nothing more seemed to occur, before it finally began a very slow and stately ascent.

Two or three years ago, I was in Paris with Mike and Geoff during a half term break. We happened to be nearby in the Avenue Bosquet and I insisted on making a detour to the Rue de Rapp. Out of curiosity, I wanted to see if the hotel was still there. I feared, of course, that it might no longer exist as a hotel or that it would have changed out of all recognition like so many places have...decharmed by some soulless modern refurbishment.

I need not have worried though. Apart from the absence of Anwar, the elderly lift attendant, who must sadly have made his final ascent to the great top floor in the sky, the hotel, including its old lift, still existed and was all just as I remembered it on that first visit to Paris.

As I drove home on New Year's Day, the morning after my night with Tina, I was in a more positive frame of mind than I had been since my father's death.

If the ancient lift at the Hotel Camélia could serve as a metaphor for my life, then I had heard the little whirring noise and I had sensed the small but perceptible quiver, even if, as yet, there was no real movement. Save for the discovery of the Delftware, nothing fundamental had really changed in my depressing circumstances, but I somehow felt that my fortunes might be about to move in an upward direction.

The button that had set off the little whirring noise and the quiver, the cause of my more hopeful mood was, of course, Tina.

I've found in life that one must always be cautious about an excess of optimism, but I had allowed myself to become, at least, a little less pessimistic.

They, those cliché-mongering bastards, those pesky purveyors of proverbs will always try to spoil things of course: first, they say: *Things can only get better.* Next, when things look as though they might indeed get better, they warn: *Not to count your chickens before they're hatched.* Then, when the chickens have actually hatched and things really are better, they tell you: *It's all too good to last.*

I wasn't, though, about to let *them,* those miserable so-and-sos, extinguish the one ray of light that had begun to shine through the darkness.

That ray of light was Tina, and our relationship had developed rapidly over the weeks in a way that I could not have dared to hope. Rather conveniently the girl, with whom she used to share, moved out, and I had more or less moved into her flat full time, only returning to my own place occasionally to check on things and pick up any post.

The up-turn in my mood was in other respects, of course, completely irrational. My parents were no more, my father's art collection had been stolen and the loss was uninsured. Furthermore, I had met with little success in finding a new job. Responses to my letters to schools and colleges, if I received any, had all been negative. I had had one interview with a school in Bristol, but that, too, was followed by one of those disheartening letters prefaced with the words 'I regret'.

Tina, however, with her unfailing cheerfulness encouraged me to be cheerful too and to believe that, whatever might happen, things would be better. Hope, if only by a small margin, had finally overtaken despair. And, of course, I had fallen in love.

❖

Not having heard anything further for some while about the investigations into the theft at Orchard House, I emailed Dennis Thrupp who, so far as I knew, was still in contact with the police. A day or two later, I received an email from him in reply to the effect that there had not been much progress, but that Chief Inspector Morgan, still in charge of the investigation, would himself be in touch with me direct, and indeed later in the same day I duly received a call from him.

He was very apologetic about the lack of any further progress but the various lines of enquiry that he had been pursuing had 'dried up', nor had Interpol yet been able to trace the man calling himself Brighella who had sold my father's Delftware collection to the shop in Amsterdam. I was assured, however, that all possible efforts to catch the criminals and recover my property would continue to be made. I made appreciative sounding noises, but privately had little confidence that much would happen.

'Oh, and one more other thing I should advise you, sir.' the Inspector added 'It's just possible that you might be contacted by the thieves themselves or somebody on their behalf...'

'What?! Why on earth?!'

'Well, sometimes, sir, professional art thieves, like the gang in this case, contact owners whose art works they've stolen and invite them basically to 'buy back' their own property...paintings, sculptures or whatever...against the threat that these things will be destroyed unless the owner agrees to a make a deal. It's a sort of ransom demand, you might say. You see, sir, thieves often encounter difficulty when asked to show due provenance, that is to say proper title, to an art work. This is especially the case with higher value items where potential buyers are obviously most concerned. Of course, the thieves may try to get over this difficulty by forging documents, but the alternative of 'ransoming' items can sometimes turn out to be the easier option, if you follow me, sir'

'Yes, I understand what you're saying.'

'Look, I honestly don't think it is very likely, sir, but if you do receive an approach along these lines from someone, you must contact me immediately. Here, I'll give you my number, if you've got a pen handy.'

I took the number down and thanked the good Inspector for his advice. I must say I didn't much like the idea of the thieves, possibly this crook Brighella or whoever he was, getting in contact with me personally to make some form of ransom demand, unlikely, though, it might be. What if they did and then found out I had no money? How might they react? Would they actually destroy some of the paintings? What could Chief Inspector Morgan realistically be able to do about it?

Altogether, the outlook on the theft issue, not to mention the job front, continued to look bleak, but the metaphorical lift was no longer quite stuck on the ground floor because of that one big new plus factor in my life, Tina.

'Do you know what?' My old friend Mike said, with just a hint of envy in his voice. 'I think you must be simultaneously the unluckiest and the luckiest man in the whole bloody world!'

CHAPTER TWENTY-TWO

Towards the end of the January, the inquest into my mother's death took place, much sooner, in fact, than Mr. Thrupp had anticipated. It turned out not be quite as intimidating as I had feared, no doubt aided by the fact that Tina had come with me to lend me her support.

The traffic warden, who had found my mother's car and the note which she had left inside it, was the first to give evidence; the note itself was read out to the court by a police officer from the local force; an image from the CCTV camera on the sea front was produced and I was called as a witness to confirm that it showed my mother which it clearly did. My mother's note was produced to me and I was asked if I recognised her handwriting, which again I was able to confirm. The next question put to me concerned the contents of the note: whether what she had written was consistent with my last conversation with her on the telephone, which indeed was the case.

I was spared any further questions about the state of my mother's relationship with my father, the changing of his will, or my mother's extra-marital affair. I would have found such questions very embarrassing and for the most part, in any case, would not have been able to give a cogent answer. After all, I had no knowledge of my mother's affair until after my father's death and didn't even know the identity of her former lover.

The main witness was of course the man, a rather charming old Irish bloke, who had seen a woman leap from the cliff edge, had witnessed her body in the water and seen her disappear beneath the surface. He was also able to recognise the image shown on the CCTV camera as the same woman, that is to say my mother.

The predictable verdict on my mother's death – *suicide while the balance of her mind was disturbed* – was duly delivered. I frankly found the whole experience rather surreal and was thankful when it was all over.

I had noticed sitting at the back of the court my mother's oldest friend in Cheltenham, Vera Johnson. It was kind of her to come to the inquest and I managed to have a few words with her as we left the court.

There was one more thing I felt I had to do – to visit the place where poor Mum had met her death, and pay my respects by casting some flowers into the sea. Outside the court, we met the nice old Irishman who was the final and principal witness and indeed the last person to see my mother alive; he said that he lived within walking distance of where it occurred and kindly agreed to take us to the spot. He had no transport and had come to the court by bus. It was the least we could do to give him a lift in the car.

We parked the car on the sea front and followed much the same route that my poor mother must have taken on her final walk. It was not too far and when we reached the place, the old man discreetly withdrew to make his way home.

We didn't climb over the iron railing protecting the path from the dangerous cliff edge. It was quite close enough for me to throw the flowers over and, as the path was in an elevated position relative to the cliff edge, I was able to watch them as they slowly drifted down into the water below and were carried away by the current. Tina put a consoling arm around my shoulders, and we stood in silence for a minute or two, before walking back to the car and heading off for home.

We had decided that evening to go for a meal at the Cotswold Tandoori, my local Indian restaurant, and spend the night for once at my flat. We went straight to the restaurant and it was quite late by the time we eventually got to bed, weary after a long day.

Tina got up early the next morning to go to work at the school, leaving me in bed. Being able to take my time over things in the mornings was, I suppose, some small consolation for having no job. After shambling about aimlessly for a bit, I finally got myself dressed and began to go through the post which I'd picked up from my box in the hall the previous night before but been too tired to look at before going to bed.

Most of it was the usual rubbish but there was another reply to one of my job enquiry letters, this time from the Headmaster of a school in Hereford beginning, of course, with those same depressing words: 'I regret'. I had only just consigned all this stuff to the wastepaper basket when the door bell sounded. It was a courier with a delivery.

With a sigh, I set off all the way down the stairs to the hall. I wasn't expecting anything and was sure that this would be some parcel for one of my neighbours out at work and that the courier man had pressed my bell in the hope that somebody would be in to whom he could entrust it. But it wasn't a parcel for someone else; it was an envelope addressed to me. Moreover, it appeared to have come from Italy.

Intrigued, I hastened back to my flat to open it. It contained a printed invitation and a letter.

I looked at the invitation first which was in Italian. It was quite a grand affair with what appeared to be a family crest embossed at the top of it. My name appeared in bold handwriting in the space provided for invitees. I pride myself that I have a natural gift for languages and had picked up a bit of Italian, encouraged my father who spoke the language well.

I was able to make sense of much of the invitation and the gist of it was that *Il Conte Alvise Bolani* – Count Alvise Bolani – was inviting me to *un ballo in maschera* – a masked ball – at a place called *Ca' Bolani* in Venice on *Martedi Grasso*.

I knew that *Martedi Grasso* meant what they call in French Mardi Gras and we call in English Shrove Tuesday or, if you prefer, Pancake Day, traditionally, the last day of feasting and fun before Lent begins. The last day, too, of the Venetian Carnival when one is supposed to bid meat – *carne*, farewell – *vale*.

Next, I turned my attention to the letter, accompanying the invitation, also embossed with the same crest. It was type-written in good English:

Dear Mr. Wilkins,

I was so sorry to learn of the death of your father, Theo, which was shortly followed, I have heard, by the death also of your mother. You have my deepest sympathy on this most dreadful double tragedy. I never had the honour of meeting your mother but I counted Theo a loyal friend. He was a most wise and cultured man.

I first met Theo many years ago at the home in England of a mutual friend and great art collector, Sir Bernard Skelton. In fact, we discovered that we had many friends and acquaintances in the art world in common, both here in Italy and in England.

Your father possessed an unsurpassed knowledge of eighteenth century Italian painting of which I myself have a modest collection. His advice to me on proposed acquisitions and on matters of valuation has been invaluable. His death will be a great loss to all collectors of fine art.

I had intended to invite your parents to my annual ball this year, and I felt that the least I could do in such sad circumstances, and as a mark of my respect for your father, would be to invite you in their place.

I very much hope that you will accept my invitation though regretfully I cannot offer to accommodate you here at Ca' Bolani as, with so many family members staying for Carnival, we have no spare room available. Fortunately, The Gritti Palace had a late cancellation and I have taken the liberty of provisionally reserving a room for you there, entirely at my expense of course, in the hopeful anticipation of your acceptance. The booking is for three nights so that you would arrive on a Monday, the day before my Ball, and depart on the following Thursday. This will at least allow you to enjoy the last day of Carnival and a day to recover after the Ball.

The dress code for the Ball is costumes and masks, but please rest assured that a suitable costume and mask will be provided for you.

I should be grateful to hear from you as soon as possible, as time is now very short. Please reply to the email address above.

I very much look forward to seeing you.

Cordiali Saluti

Yours most sincerely,

Alvise Bolani

Now, anyone would think that I'd be overjoyed to receive such an invitation, but my first thought was the warning Chief Inspector Morgan had given me when we spoke on the telephone. Could this be some form of trap? Did Count Bolani really exist or, if he did, was this invitation from an imposter posing as Count Bolani? The invitation card and letter could be fakes.

Might I arrive in Venice only to be met by some shaven-headed, barrel-chested thug in expensive shades, by whom I would be strong-armed, bundled into a fast motor launch and whisked away to some remote island in the Venetian lagoon, where the suave but sinister Signor Brighella would issue an extortionate ransom demand in relation to my father's paintings – and with terrible consequences to follow if payment wasn't forthcoming, both for the paintings and probably for me too?

I searched for Count Bolani on the internet. There was a fair amount of information on the Bolani family, plainly of ancient and noble origin, and it was true that the present Count was called Alvise. There was an image too of Ca' Bolani, a beautiful pink wedding cake-like palace on the Grand Canal in the Venetian Gothic style, which was indeed the family home. The Bolani Ball, held each year on *Martedi Grasso,* marking the end of the Venetian Carnival, also received a mention.

Of course, a crook could easily have gleaned enough information to fake the invitation and letter from various sources. Even Sir Bernard Skelton was referred to in my father's obituary in *The Times*.

However, the information on the website, coupled with the quality of the Invitation card and the content and tone of the letter, convinced me of their authenticity. More to the point, why should the thieves go to such elaborate lengths? Why not simply contact me at home if they wished to make a ransom demand?

Clearly, I thought, I'd allowed my over-active imagination to run away with me. Calm down, I told myself, there's no problem; it's all above board.

I phoned Tina at the school office and briefly told her all about it. She was dismissive of any cause for concern.

'You must go, William' She said 'It'll be a wonderful adventure!'

'Yes, I suppose it will be' The word 'adventure' generally alarmed me, but this would not be the sort of madcap affair of the kind Mike might suggest. This would be a truly civilised experience, I told myself.

'But I shall miss you, Tina, miss you a lot, you know.' I said.

'Don't be silly, William. You're going for three days not three months.'

'All right then' I said 'I'll go; I'll accept right now.'

As soon as I'd finished speaking to Tina, I emailed my acceptance as required by Count Bolani's letter, and felt good about it. I'd been To Venice several times before, but it was not one of those places of which one says 'Well, I've been there, done that'; it's a place to which one never minds returning, time and time again...And this promised to be a very special visit indeed.

I'd only just made myself a cup of coffee and sat down with my laptop to explore the internet for a cheap flight to Venice, when the telephone rang. It was Dennis Thrupp.

I thought he might be calling with some news, good or bad about the paintings, but it was something else.

Maurice Beckman & partners' solicitors had been in touch with him. Their clients had decided to put Orchard House up for sale, retaining only the gallery on the ground floor on a lease-back arrangement. The deal with my father, however, provided for a six month period of grace for the property to be vacated, much of which was still to run. If I would agree to vacate by no later than, say, the end of February, which would involve, of course, removing all the furniture, fittings and belongings, Beckmans would be prepared to make a compensation payment of £1500.

Mr. Thrupp thought he could get them up to £2000 if I would accept their proposal. After a little more discussion, I said I would agree to it on the basis of a compensation figure of £2000 as he had suggested, and I instructed him to proceed accordingly.

After my conversation with Mr. Thrupp came to an end, I sat down to drink my coffee and was about to resume my search for a flight when the telephone rang again.

'Is that Mr. William Wilkins?' A man's voice enquired in a very plummy accent.

'Speaking.'

'This is Jeremy Babbington here of Fitzroy Elite Travel Services. I gather you are travelling to Venice on Monday week, returning on the following Thursday.'

'Yes, that's right.'

'Count Alvise Bolani has asked me to arrange flights for you. Availability is rather limited at present, but I have managed to secure a seat in Business Class on British Airways from Heathrow for both outgoing and return flights on the required dates.'

'Business class!'

'Well, the Count would hardly expect a guest of his to travel 'steerage', old boy!'

'Yes but the cost!'

'My dear fellow, the Count will naturally be paying your fare. You have no need to concern yourself with that. Now, if you will let me have your email address, date of birth and passport details, I will provide you shortly with all the relevant flight information. There will of course be an E-ticket.'

I spent the next eleven days or so in eager anticipation of my Venice adventure. I must say I was greatly looking forward to it. I knew that the Gritti Palace was one of the great hotels of Venice, a byword for elegance. It was here, in fact, that my parents had spent their honeymoon. Tina had even insisted that I bought, out of my slender resources, a smart new jacket and trousers for the occasion.

Then, of course, there was the masked ball to be held at the private palazzo of an ancient and noble Venetian family, which promised to be a once in a lifetime experience.

And the wonderful thing was that everything, absolutely everything, it appeared, would be entirely without cost to me. The whole thing seemed utterly fantastic...and that is perhaps why there lurked in the darker recesses of my mind just a tiny niggle of doubt that all might not be quite as it seemed.

CHAPTER TWENTY-THREE

I spent the night before my flight to Venice with 'Bad Uncle' Charles at his house just outside Windsor, conveniently close to Heathrow. When I arrived, there was a young woman there, whom Uncle introduced as his secretary, at which she blushed, not quite managing to stifle a little giggle. Indeed, there didn't seem to be much in the way of what one might describe as secretarial services going on and in any case it was a Sunday, but then 'secretarial services' plainly had a broad definition so far as uncle was concerned. She too stayed the night.

Next morning I took a taxi to the airport arriving in absurdly good time, checked in and dropped off my hold luggage. With my Business Class ticket I found I was able to use a private lounge and happily avoid the scrum of suffering humanity in the main departure hall. I felt very superior, trying to forget that by comparison with others using the lounge, I was more or less a pauper.

Nothing remains perfect for long, though. Having settled myself in a comfortable seat with a coffee, I had just begun to read the day's paper when one of those thrusting business types came to sit next to me. He was wearing a smart suit, or perhaps 'sharp' would be a better word for it: more designer label than bespoke; no tie of course. He extracted his laptop from an expensive-looking leather slipcase, fiddled with it a bit and put it away again. Next, he produced his mobile phone and proceeded to call a colleague. I obviously couldn't hear what the colleague was saying, but what I could hear of the conversation was conducted almost entirely in management speak:

'Hi, Phil, how does our strategic staircase look?

'Good, but we're still behind the curve. Got to action the pre-plan as of now.

'Yeah, get all the ducks in a row; tick all the boxes.

'Sure thing! Going forward, we must implement full-on matrix management.'

'Let's have more thought showers; blue sky thinking sessions.'

'Too right, Phil, it's on my radar.'

'Yeah, brilliant! Why not appoint Ted our product evangelist?

'With the right paradigm shift, Phil, we can really push the envelope!'

Mercifully, before I had to listen to any more of this dreadful drivel, the bloke's flight for Frankfurt was called; he picked up his case and left, his phone still clasped to his ear.

There was still some time to go before my flight, and having read all I wanted to read in the newspaper, I took out from my small rucksack a book I had brought with me about Venetian masks and costumes which my father had given me on his return from one of his trips to Italy.

Masks and costumes for the Venetian carnival, I read, fall into two broad categories:

First, traditional masks and costumes, many, though not all, of which derive from the Commedia dell'Arte and its stock characters – for example, Harlequin, Pulcinella, Colombina. These, of course, are not solely associated with the Carnival or indeed with Venice. They crop up wherever Commedia dell'Arte theatre is performed, but they were, and are to this day, commonly to be seen during the Venetian carnival time.

Secondly, modern masks and costumes, usually zany and colourful creations, sometimes with a passing resemblance to traditional forms but often quite original.

I started to thumb through the book, looking at the glossy colour pictures, to remind myself about them. About half way through, I came upon one depicting a figure wearing a loose white tunic and baggy trousers, each striped with green braid, and an olive green half mask with wide eye-holes and a hooked nose. In his right hand, he carried a sort of baton. I looked at the caption beneath the picture; it read:

> Brighella (origin: Bergamo), a roguish jack of all trades, one
> of the original Zani (comic servants) of the Commedia
> dell'Arte. He often, like Harlequin, carries a wooden stick or
> baton called in Venetian dialect a batocio.

Brighella! I knew when the name was mentioned in connection with the Delftware saga, I'd seen it before somewhere, but I couldn't think where. Well, as expected, Dennis Thrupp was right. That Italian rogue in Amsterdam certainly gave a false name, but what a cheeky one to choose!

I had no time to ponder the matter further as my flight to Venice was called.

CHAPTER TWENTY-FOUR

The flight was all very smooth and comfortable, and indeed we arrived slightly ahead of schedule which was all to the good, but my bag failed to materialise on the carousel until almost all the other passengers have collected theirs, and I became quite convinced that it had been routed in error to Dar es Salaam or somewhere. Eventually, though, it emerged, alone and forlorn-looking like an abandoned child; one of its wheels was missing, of course.

I had intended to take the Alilaguna water bus from the airport to Piazza San Marco as I had done on my previous visit. It takes time, but it's a good way to go; approaching Venice from the water is infinitely more romantic than going by road to the Piazzale Roma and the Gritti Palace is not too far to walk from San Marco, even with a damaged wheelie case.

However, as I was soon to find out, other transport had been arranged for me.

Immediately outside Arrivals there were a row of people holding up cards with the names of passengers whom they were there to meet off the London flight. Amongst them was a man holding up a card with my name on it. He was a short, stocky, man with a weather-beaten face wearing a broad smile. I couldn't really believe that he was in the employ of a ruthless criminal gang intent on kidnap.

'Buongiorno, Signore,' he said. 'I am Marcello. I 'ope you 'ad a safe flight.

'Safe? Well, I suppose so. After all, I got here. The thing didn't crash into Mont Blanc or anything.'

'Mi dispiace – I beg pardon?'

'Sorry, sorry,' I said 'Excuse my flippancy.'

'Che?' His face puckered in a frown. Another of those mad

Englishmen, I could see him thinking, not without some justification.

'I mean the flight was very good... very comfortable... very safe'

'Oh, bene, bene' he said, the smile instantly re-appearing, 'Now, please to follow me to my boat. I take you Gritti Palace, vero?'

He insisted on carrying both my bag and rucksack and we walked together from the terminal to where his water taxi, a comfortable motor launch, was moored. In a moment or two, we were on our way, and, with a deep throaty roar, we whooshed off towards Venice hazily visible in the distance.

Entering Venice by, I believe, the Rio di Santa Giustina near the Hospital, we weaved our way round through various canals, passing the magnificent church of San Giorgio dei Greci with its leaning tower, eventually to emerge onto that part of the lagoon known as the Canale di San Marco. Proceeding in parallel to the Riva degli Schiavoni, and passing between the Island of San Giorgio Maggiore and the Doges' Palace, the launch soon arrived at the entrance to the Grand Canal with the great baroque bulk of the church of La Salute, the Grande Dame of the Canal, on our port side. We progressed only a little further before the launch slowed to a crawling speed, and manoeuvred in towards a large building.

'Siamo arrivati' said Marcello 'This is your hotel, Signor Wilkins, The Gritti Palace.'

The Gritti Palace. A few weeks ago, I could scarcely have dreamt it, but now here I was. Wonderful!

My room exceeded all expectations for elegance and comfort, not to mention the magnificent views from the window up and down the Grand Canal, with La Salute diagonally opposite.

At the foot of the bed, there was a large cardboard box, on the top of which had been scrawled in black felt-tip pen 'Sgr. Wilkins'. I opened it. It was a traditional chequered Harlequin costume complete with a funny floppy hat and a black and red diamond pattern mask: my costume for the Ball, just as the Count had promised. It was no cheap fancy dress outfit either but had been beautifully made of the finest materials, probably a replica of an eighteenth-century original.

Before doing anything further, I decided to try it on, worried that it might not fit me, but it did, like a glove – good! I put on the hat and mask, went into the bathroom, and preened myself in front of the mirror. Thoroughly satisfied, I took everything off again, and restored the whole lot to the box. The business-class flight, private water taxi from the airport, the Gritti Palace, and now this splendid Harlequin costume – everything was going absolutely swimmingly, wasn't it? That tiny niggle of doubt had all but disappeared, almost.

After finishing unpacking my bag, I decided to take a walk to re-acquaint myself with the city. It was a fine clear day and the weather was quite mild – perfect for walking.

A short stroll took me to Piazza San Marco, where there was of course a great throng of people, many in masks and costumes of all sorts. Quite a few, I noticed, were wearing what is called the 'Bauta', some just the mask and hat, others in full costume.

The Bauta is a white mask covering the whole face and is distinguished by a large protruding beak-like chin, allowing the wearer to eat and drink without having to remove it. Though not one stemming from the Commedia dell'Arte tradition, it is the most common of the traditional Venetian masks and its use was not limited in the eighteenth century to carnival time. In fact, the Bauta came to refer not only to the mask but to the whole costume which goes with it consisting of a long black silk cloak with a cape of black silk lace suspended from a black tricorn hat. The whole effect of the mask and costume is to lend its wearer a slightly sinister air of mystery. Its purpose was essentially one of disguise and it was also a great social leveller as it could be worn by people of high or low birth, by Venetians or foreign visitors, by men or sometimes even women. Indeed, one could not tell whether you had just encountered a prince or a tradesman, Casanova himself or the lady he had just seduced.

I had thought of stopping for a coffee at one of the celebrated cafes on either side of the piazza, but it was all too busy, so I walked on past the Doges' Palace and along the Riva degli Schiavoni, the wide walkway by the lagoon.

As I passed, I took a sideways glance at the Ponte Dei Sospiri, the famous Bridge of Sighs, the bridge across which convicted prisoners made a one way journey from the Doges Palace to the gloomy dungeons on the other side. It struck me that my life, at least until recently, had also been a one way ticket to gloom, but not wishing to dwell on this unhelpful analogy, I marched resolutely on until, after a short distance, I took a turn to the left and made my way to the square called Campo San Zaccaria. Since I was there, I thought I might as well take the opportunity to explore the church and take a quick look at the renowned altarpiece by Giovanni Bellini, which my father so much admired but which I'd never seen before.

After San Zaccaria, feeling rather pleased with myself after my dose of culture, I meandered through the maze of little calle, along fondamenta by the side of canals, and over small bridges, bringing me eventually to the lovely Campo Santa Maria Formosa. Walking on from there, I soon arrived at the Campo Santi Giovanni e Paolo where I stopped at a café for a rest and a refreshing Spritz con Aperol.

Having refreshed myself and paid the bill, I set off once more, planning to return, at a slower pace, to the hotel by a different route.

I had not gone far and had stopped momentarily on a bridge over a small canal to take in the view. I looked first in one direction, and, before moving on, turned round to look up the other way. It was then that I saw it, the *figure* I mean, standing in the middle of the next little bridge along and wearing a Bauta.

It was now quite late in the day and it was beginning to grow dark, but I could still see fairly clearly as the bridge on which the figure was standing was illuminated by a light shining through the window of an adjoining building. I had already, of course, seen many people dressed up in a Bauta costume not only in St. Mark's Square but elsewhere too on my walk, but this figure, whoever he was, was *staring* at *me*, at *me personally*. I was sure of it. Although the figure was some way off, the intensity of the stare through the eye-holes in the mask was to me quite palpable. We all possess some form of sixth sense which defies logical explanation, and mine told me, at that moment as I stood in the fading light of that late afternoon in Venice, that I was being closely observed by a sinister figure on the next bridge, who both knew me, and wanted something of me. But who, what, why?

I averted my gaze, and hastily walked down off the bridge, but as I passed between two buildings into a narrow calle , I could not stop myself from looking back again towards the bridge on which the figure had been standing. There was no-one there. I quickened my pace, until I came out onto a busier thoroughfare, not far from the Rialto Bridge. Soon, I reached Campo San Bartolomeo, where there was a great crowd of people. Re-assured, I suppose, by the surrounding presence of the crowd, I began to feel less disturbed by my recent experience, indeed to dismiss it as a bit of nonsense.

After pausing a while in the campo, I continued walking, allowing myself to be driven along with the flow of people making their way in the direction of San Marco. I stopped to look in the window of a shoe shop, and was admiring a pair of rather stylish shoes, when I saw the Bauta figure again, this time reflected in the glass of the shop window quite close and again appearing to look at me directly. It was only a fleeting glimpse in the passing crowds, but somehow I was quite certain that it was the same person. I turned round but he had gone, swallowed up already by the enveloping tide of humanity making its laborious shuffling progress along the street. Try as I might, I couldn't restrain a sense of, well, foreboding, I suppose, ridiculous and irrational as I tried to persuade myself it was.

My intended return route to the hotel involved missing out Piazza

San Marco, but this would entail passing through quieter areas and I didn't fancy another encounter with my ghostly friend on some dimly-lit calle. So I decided after all to keep with the crowds and go via St. Mark's Square and thereafter follow the route in the direction of the Accademia Bridge which passes close to the Gritti. As I walked I tried to persuade myself again that all this was rubbish - the figure on the bridge, if indeed he was not completely a product of my fevered mind, was simply someone in a mask enjoying the view down the canal as I had done. The reflection in the window of the shop was almost certainly of someone else entirely. Don't be so stupid.

I had almost convinced myself when, with a sigh of relief, I turned into the small campo with the entrance to the Gritti Palace towards the end of it on the left, close to a little landing point for gondolas lurching up and down in their peculiar cork-screw motion with the choppiness of the water.

As I was about to enter the hotel, I caught sight of something out of the corner of my eye. I didn't want to look but, out of some inner compulsion, I couldn't help myself. Thank God! It was only a group of masked and costumed women...wonderful modern ones too, all blue and gold, of a fantastical design, and crowned with enormous matching head-wear and exquisitely painted masks...certainly an eye-catching sight, but at least not a frightening or threatening one. They had stopped at the top end of the campo to let a Japanese tourist take their picture. Flash! Flash!

I watched them move off in the direction of the Accademia, but as they did so... Oh, Christ! Standing right behind the place where they had posed for their picture to be taken was *It*, that masked and cloaked figure again, again *staring, staring* through those hollow eyes, *staring at me*.

I stood staring back, rooted to the spot, unable to move.

'Sorry, old chap' a very English voice said. The owner of the voice, on his way out of the hotel, had bumped into me as I stood in his way. He, too, was dressed in a Bauta costume, and I nearly jumped out of my skin.

'Sorry' I said, as I staggered to move out of his way. When I looked back up the length of the campo, the figure had gone. I went into the hotel foyer. My hands were shaking and I must have looked as white as a sheet. The Head Porter asked me if I was feeling all right, and two elderly guests looked concerned. I had intended to go straight to my room, but instead I made my way to the elegant Longhi Bar named after the very painter who had painted that superb set of four paintings that had belonged to my father. I ordered a Bellini cocktail which I knocked back very quickly; then I ordered another which I sipped rather more slowly, and tried to take a rational view of my recent experiences.

I was clearly allowing my obsessive mind to invent things, to tilt at proverbial windmills, I assured myself. There must be hundreds of people dressed up in the Bauta costume at Carnival time, after all. What I had seen were three *different* people in different places; the first, perhaps an English visitor like me; the second, may be, a proud Venetian pleased with all the trade that these foreign visitors brought to the city, but slightly contemptuous of them nonetheless; the last one, near the hotel, perhaps an innocent hausfrau from Dortmund or somewhere trying to enter into the spirit of carnival; who could say?...And, of course, if they were facing in my general direction, the rather frightening masks would make it look as if they were staring at me. It was all such rubbish – I must put it out of head.

Feeling even better after spending some time luxuriating in the bath and changing into the new jacket and trousers which Tina had wisely made me buy, I progressed to the dining room to enjoy a truly splendid dinner for which I imagined that my generous host Count Bolani would be picking up the tab.

I must say I felt slightly guilty afterwards, particularly as I'd ordered some rather expensive wine to go with my dinner. Not so guilty, however, as to prevent me from visiting the bar once more for a Grappa as a final night-cap.

In my pleasantly woozy state, the Bauta figure had entirely passed from my mind. But I had no idea what was to follow next day.

CHAPTER TWENTY-FIVE

When I awoke in the morning it took some moments for me to come to terms with reality –Was I really staying at the Gritti Palace on the Grand Canal in Venice and going that evening to a masked ball at another palace? With some effort I levered myself out of the comfortable bed and opened the shutters to a morning of hazy sunshine and pale blue sky. A low-lying mist hung over the Grand Canal, a scene reminiscent of an impressionist painting. Was all this just an impression then, a dream? Would I wake up in a moment or two to find myself in my attic flat in Gloucestershire? Suddenly a waterbus, or vaporetto as it is known in Venice, chugged into view full of people. Reality had broken in – yes, it was indeed all true!

I couldn't resist trying on the Harlequin costume again, and I even entertained the idea of wearing it all day, but thought better of it and replaced it carefully in its box.

It was still quite chilly when I set out after breakfast, but soon it became sunnier and warmer and the early mist melted away.

I spent the day wandering about with no particular plan. Venice is just about the best place in the world for aimless wandering and a place where getting lost, which of course I did, is a not a matter of concern but of pleasure.

As I was returning to the Gritti palace at the end of a long and enjoyable day, I passed through the Campo Santo Stefano, one of the largest and most beautiful squares in Venice. Like St Mark's Square the day before, it was full of people, many of them costumed or, at least, wearing masks.

I was passing close to a group of ladies in authentic eighteenth-century dress with small black masks, when a man suddenly appeared from nowhere dressed in a Brighella costume. He seemed to be staring at me as the Bauta figure yesterday had done. Was this

'Signor. Brighella' the brazen thief, last seen In Amsterdam, out to kidnap me? No, no I assured myself, nonsense! I nevertheless quickened my pace, occasionally looking over my shoulder to see if I was being followed. It was with some relief that I arrived at the welcoming entrance to the hotel.

Safely back, I was just about to go up to my room when the receptionist stopped me.

'Signor Wilkins, Count Bolani's Secretary telephoned with a message, a gondola will be ready to take you to Ca' Bolani at a quarter past seven. Please to be outside in the campo by this time.'

'Oh, I see… yes, thank you.'

Well, well, a gondola to take me to the Ball. How very thoughtful of them, I thought. In the course of my wanderings the previous day, I had discovered where The Ca' Bolani was and thought I knew how to get there but I had not been entirely relishing the prospect of a walk in the dark with the quite likely possibility of missing my way. Well, now there would be no danger of getting lost - And what a wonderful prospect: to arrive by gondola! A real gilding of a lily already well-gilded, but I didn't know then what was to come.

I was ready outside by the water's edge in the campo on the dot of quarter past seven. Though I say so myself, I looked absolutely splendid in my Harlequin costume, and I saw other guests casting admiring glances in my direction. Altogether, I was greatly looking forward to the evening.

'Signor Wilkins?' A gondolier asked.

'Yes, that's me.'

'Thees way, please.'

I was shown to one of the gondolas moored nearby on the Grand

Canal. The gondolier helped me aboard, and I was just settling myself on the cushioned seat nearest to the stern of the craft, when there was a clattering of running feet and two figures suddenly appeared out of the darkness.

The first was a large man and he was dressed as Brighella. Brighella, by God! There must have been other Brighellas in Venice that evening – why should I believe that this one was the man calling himself Brighella who had sold my father's Delftware in Amsterdam? I did though. That wretched sixth sense of mine told me so, and from his physique I was sure, too, that he was the same man that I'd seen not long before in Campo Santo Stefano.

As if to compound my fears, the figure following on behind him was dressed in a Bauta costume and mask, and I was sure beyond doubt that it was the very same sinister figure I'd seen the day before, the one on that bridge staring at me, the same person indeed as the one reflected in the shop window and the same one who'd given me such a fright near the hotel. I had deluded myself yesterday into believing that I was mistaken, that there was nothing in all this, nothing to worry about. My logic had been impeccable, but wrong – In my bones, I knew that now.

Nodding to the gondolier, the two of them clambered aboard the gondola and seated themselves together at the forward end. Before I could think what to do, the gondolier had cast off and using his oar pushed us out from the bank.

'Good evening, Gentleman. We meet again' I said, with as much insouciance as I could muster. Neither said anything in reply, but whispered to each other in low voices. They knew who I was all right. Indeed, I thought I detected half a smile from Brighella, though his mouth was only just visible below his mask.

The gondolier passed round some warm rugs for us to wrap around ourselves. The night was clear but very cold. Brighella cast his aside with a gesture of contempt, and it was hastily taken up by the Bauta person in addition to the one already allocated. Gratefully, I took mine, though it failed to stop my teeth from chattering, but the chattering had in my case much more to do with fear than cold. Clearly this was a hi-jacking. I wasn't meant to go to any Ball. The message supposedly from Count Bolani's secretary was a pretence; it had obviously come from these rogues. The gondolier must be in their pay. At any moment I felt sure the gondola would turn aside from the Grand Canal into one of the quiet smaller canals... then they'd make their ransom demand for my father's paintings just as the Chief Inspector had warned.

What would they do when I told them I had no money? Would they believe me or would they not? Would they take me away to some secret hideaway and lock me in a windowless room? Or would they come to the conclusion that I was no use to them, in which case would they let me go free? Unlikely. No it would be *Death in Venice* for me. They'd pounce on me, truss me up like the proverbial chicken, weigh me down with chains or something, and throw me into the cold dark waters. My only hope would be to jump out before they could get hold of me and swim for it. I should have enjoyed my journey in the gondola; it should have been one of the highpoints of my visit to Venice. Instead I spent it in abject fear, trying to calculate when I should make my move, nervously watching my travelling companions, and feeling like a helpless vole on a motorway verge as hawks hovered above waiting to swoop.

But nothing happened. There was an anxious moment when the gondola suddenly veered closer towards the bank. Apprehensively, I looked up and down expecting to see a little canal come into view into which the gondola would turn, but instead, there, only thirty yards away, was the Ca' Bolani in all its pink splendour with its elaborate gothic tracery and ogee-arched windows. The gondola edged towards a quay with steps leading up from the water's edge to an old wooden doorway flanked by a giant pair of wrought-iron lamps. Two flunkies, bewigged and dressed as eighteenth-century footmen, waited to help guests as they came ashore and check their names against the guest list. A large contingent of boisterous Italians had just arrived in a water taxi, in a dazzling array of costumes.

Another gondola was behind us. After the taxi had gone, we were next in line. Brighella and the Bauta figure were helped out first and disappeared quickly inside the building. I followed more slowly, breathing a heavy sigh of relief.

So there it was, I concluded, my vivid imagination had yet again got the better of me.

Once inside, I joined a large crowd of people merging from my left having arrived by the street entrance from the adjoining calle. We all made our way sedately up a substantial marble stairway to the piano nobile where a wide landing led, through an impressive set of double doors, into a grand ballroom. Whilst the Ca' Bolani dated from the fourteenth century, much of the interior had been given a rococo makeover in the eighteenth century and both walls and ceilings of the salon were embellished with wonderful frescoes by Tiepolo or his contemporaries mainly of hunting or pastoral scenes. A series of exquisite rococo mirrors and enormous Murano glass chandeliers completed the rich ornamentation.

Tables had been set out in the ballroom, each beautifully laid out for dinner with meticulous detail and each with its own set of magnificent silver candlesticks. A large space had been left in the centre presumably for dancing at a later stage of the evening.

I gave my name to another flunkey who led me to a table by a window where I had a superb view of the Grand Canal with the Rialto Bridge in the distance. I shared the table with a party of friendly Italians from Verona who were related in some way to the Count. Looking around as I took my place, I noticed several people in the room dressed in the Bauta costume, though most had removed their masks and capes. I was unable, however, to detect anywhere the two characters who had shared my gondola.

During the course of the excellent meal, served by a team of yet more flunkeys in a different but equally smart livery, a small string orchestra played a selection of Venetian baroque music by Vivaldi, Albinoni and Tartini. The whole glittering event was simply magical. My earlier encounter on the gondola I had now all but forgotten.

As the coffee arrived after the final course, the senior flunkey, or major domo as perhaps I ought to call him, announced in both English and Italian that dancing would shortly commence. The string orchestra had already given way to a modern band of some sort. Having no partner with me, I thought I might as well remain seated where I was and continue to enjoy the lovely view from the window.

I had only just drained the last drop of coffee, however, when a man appeared at my elbow. He was dressed more soberly in a black costume like some eighteenth-century clerk or functionary. Indeed, that is essentially what he was, for he introduced himself as the Count's secretary and advised that the Count himself would like to see me in the library. Perhaps I would follow him, he asked politely. I was led away through the crowd of people in the ballroom and from there, via the landing, to another grand stairway leading up to the floor above. On the way there, I noticed that almost available every inch of wall space was covered by paintings, mainly of the same genre and period as those which had formed the core of my father's collection.

We reached the top of the stairs, walked on for some distance along a wide landing like that of the piano nobile below, and presently came to another grand set of double doors. The secretary knocked deferentially before opening one of the doors and standing aside to let me pass through.

CHAPTER TWENTY-SIX

I entered a large, softly lit, elegant room. Along each of the walls, there were a series of massive bookcases, each topped with carved oriental-style pinnacles in the same exotic form as those crowning the front elevation of the palazzo itself. In the centre of the room, there was a giant desk, on both sides of which stood a standard lamp, each with an elaborate wrought iron base and a shade finished in some fabric woven and fashioned in the shape of a large shield with its centre embroidered with what I recognised as the Bolani family crest. Two magnificent glass chandeliers, like those in the ballroom below, lent a final touch of splendour to this great room.

Behind the desk, with its lavishly patterned inlay work, squatted an enormous throne-like chair, three smaller versions of which faced the desk on the opposite side. Seated at the desk, in the great chair, was a man dressed as 'Il dottore della peste', the plague doctor. This took the form of a black gown and a white mask with a very long curved beak like a bird.

This must be Count Bolani, I thought, and so indeed it was. As I approached, he removed the mask and rose to his feet to greet me.

'Good evening, Signor Wilkins. Welcome to Ca' Bolani. Permit me to introduce myself: I have the honour to be your host, this evening, Alvisse Bolani. I hope you are enjoying our Ball.' The Count spoke flawless English with hardly the trace of an accent.

'Oh, yes, very much' I said, trying not to betray a nervousness brought on by that troubling sixth sense of mine.

'I always wear this costume at carnival time.' The Count continued. 'In times of old, doctors often wore a long beak mask to ward off infection, but now it is the odour of cheap tourism and filthy fast food against which protection is needed. Now, do you recognise the pictures?'

'Pictures?'

'Look' the Count said, pointing to the far end of the room.

I turned to look as I was bidden and there each placed on an easel of its own and illuminated by spotlights were four paintings of domestic scenes in eighteenth-century Venice by Pietro Longhi, the set of four paintings which had belonged to my father.

So that was it. This *was* a trap after all. The Count himself must himself be the leader of the criminal gang of art thieves who'd stolen my inheritance. He was the Big Boss, the Mastermind, il Capo, all along. I should have guessed.

I turned back again to face him.

'Don't worry.' He said, smiling and motioning me to one of the chairs by the desk. 'All will become clear to you very shortly, but first, there is someone I should like you to meet.'

I sat down, my hands trembling with apprehension.

Just beyond the desk and behind the Count's chair there was a large floor screen with panels each decorated with oriental scenes, and as the Count spoke, a figure emerged from behind it. It was, without the slightest doubt, the Bauta figure again; the same one who'd stared at me from the little bridge; the same one who'd shared the gondola on the way to the Ball.

He advanced slowly, moving around the desk, towards where I was sitting. As he did so, he cast aside the long black cape.

But it wasn't a man – it was a woman, a woman in a beautiful, lacy ball gown.

As she came level with my chair, she stood for a moment or two looking down at me.

Finally, she removed the sinister mask.

The woman looking down on me was my mother.

I gasped and tried to say something, but no words would come.

Mother bent down and delicately kissed me.

'Hello, William.' She said. 'I think I owe you an explanation.'

I gurgled incoherently, struggling to regain control of my tongue. 'But, but...you're dead, Mum' I just managed to say.

'Well, I'll explain all that in a moment, but let's start from the beginning, usually the best place to start.' She said, pulling up a chair to sit next to me.

'As I wrote in my 'suicide note', Theo and I had not been getting on well. He was very moody, much worse than usual. Frankly, I think he was unwell, but I didn't realize that at the time. When we spoke, which was not very often, we argued, arguments which became more pointless but ever more acrimonious as time went by.

'I was feeling unloved and unwanted, but one day a man came into the shop where I used to work part-time. His name was Roberto, Roberto Trevisan, an antique dealer from Treviso, near here'.

Mother turned to face the floor screen.

'Roberto,' she called, 'Come and join us.'

The man dressed as Brighella, the man I'd seen in Campo Santo Stefano, the man in the gondola, came out from behind the screen. He'd already removed his mask and I could see that he was a distin-guished-looking man about the same age as my mother. I had no doubt that he was the one who had sold the Delftware in Amster-dam. He came over to me and, smiling, shook my hand before seating himself on the remaining available chair.

'Roberto has a sister, married to an Englishman, who lives in Gloucester' Mother continued. 'He comes to England for a month or so in the winter season and travels up and down the country to auction sales and antique shops, sometimes selling stuff he's brought over with him, but more often buying things to take back to sell in Italy. He uses his sister's place as a base.

'He'd visited the shop a couple of times before but never, till then, when I'd been there. We had a good long chat and he bought a handsome pair of Regency candelabra which I let him have at a very cheap price.'

'Non e vero. Ees not true!' Roberto piped up. 'She rob me, but I pay anyway because she so beautiful!'

'Well,' mother continued ignoring Roberto's interruption, 'we'd got on so well that I suggested we meet up for a coffee later. After that, we arranged to see each other again, and, to cut a long story short, we began an affair. He was supposed to be going back to Italy, but he stayed on. At first we were very discreet, but then we did something very stupid.

'Theo went up to London from time to time to put in an appearance at the gallery there as he was obliged to do under his consultancy agreement with Maurice Beckman. Usually, on these occasions he stayed up for a night or two at his club. On one such occasion, I invited Roberto to stay overnight at Orchard House. It was a reckless thing to do. I needn't go into the precise details, but Theo found out.

'As I said in the suicide note, we had a terrible row and things went from bad to worse. Not only did he say that he was changing his will, but he threatened me with divorce. The final straw came when I overheard a conversation he was having on the telephone in which he was discussing with someone the idea of moving his art collection elsewhere. He was saying that I was mad, that he wouldn't put it past me to slash a canvas out of spite and that he wanted to put the paintings beyond my reach – Well, really!

'I was as furious with him as he was with me, but I think I had more right to be angry. I'd married him when I was very young and I'd supported him through good times and bad – and they were bad, I can tell you, during the financial crash. I had acted effectively as his unpaid secretary for years, I had helped him build up his precious art collection and regarded it as much mine as his. Our lives were, in every sense, a joint enterprise.

'It was clear to me that our relationship was beyond repair. If he chose to divorce me, I knew I would probably get some sort of court settlement, but why should I suffer the agony of going through all that.

'Roberto had now come into my life. He gave me the sympathy

and support I needed and I realised that I was falling, had fallen, in love with him and I sensed the feeling was mutual.

'But what was I to do?

'Well, it so happened that, at about this time, I heard on the local news that a country house nearby had been burgled, some valuable paintings had been stolen and that the police suspected that this was the work of an international gang of art thieves. There had apparently been a series of similar thefts in the Thames Valley and Cotswold areas over the preceding four months. This set me thinking, and after discussing it all with Roberto, we hit upon a plan.

'During one of his absences in London, we'd load up Roberto's van with all Theo's pictures and his Delftware and disappear. We'd make it look like a break-in and the police would think it was yet another heist by this gang of art thieves who were active in the area.

'As you know, the lane at the back of Orchard House is nicely concealed on both sides by high walls and Orchard House is the last house at the end furthest from the main road, so it was unlikely that anyone would see us.'

'But why the suicide?' I butted in.

'Well, if we simply disappeared at the same time as Orchard House was burgled, it would look too much of a coincidence for the police to ignore. They would be bound to consider whether this was really the work of the gang or not. They would inevitably suspect that I was involved, with or without others, or even that I had colluded with the gang for a share of the proceeds. At the very least, they would have to investigate the alternative possibilities. That's why we came up with the fake suicide idea. It suited me, too. I wanted to draw a line under my old life and start a new one, totally afresh. I didn't want anyone trying to find me.'

'Even me?' I asked.

'Yes, even you, William, though I did have the vague notion that one day, when the dust had all settled, I would try to make contact with you again.'

'But surely when Dad died, things were different...'

'Well, I must say that I wavered. The plan was put on hold, and I was thinking of talking to you, but then we had that dreadful conversation after you met Dennis Thrupp, and I thought to hell with it, we're going ahead. We were all ready to go and the wheels were set in motion the very next day.'

'Mum, I didn't mean what I said and I should have been prepared to listen to you but I was very upset.'

'Of course, you were upset. I don't blame you at all, not now...but at the time I was not in the mood. I knew, if I stayed I could probably have contested the will, but why bother?!'

'You said in your suicide note that your affair was short-lived, that it was over.'

'I know, but, as you can see, that was a lie. I felt I had to say that because it might look a bit odd otherwise. If I still had a lover, why kill myself?'

'I still don't get how you faked the suicide...Some old Irish gent saw you jump off the cliff and sinking under the waves and he gave evidence at the inquest.'

'Yes, that was Liam Kelly, but he never saw any such thing. Liam was my father's oldest friend. They played golf twice a week and went sailing together. He's known me since I was a baby. Liam would do anything for me. We had made up this story for him to tell, and he was primed and ready whenever we gave the word. I'm sure he told it well with that special gift for story-telling that the Irish have.'

'He certainly did!'

'Well, we carried out our burglary at Orchard House, doing a bit of damage in the process to make it look real. Having loaded up Roberto's van, we drove down to Cocklemouth, he in the van and I in my car, arriving quite late. I made sure to park the car badly in a place where it would soon be found next morning. After parking, I walked down to the sea-front and then along the promenade towards the cliffs, making sure that I would be picked up on the CCTV. Once I got to the cliff path, I didn't continue round to the place I was supposed to have jumped, but took another path leading directly to Liam's cottage where Roberto was waiting for me.

'The next day we drove to Dover and took the ferry to Ostend, with me hidden in the back of the van just in case. From Ostend we drove on up to Amsterdam. Some of Theo's Delftware was really quite valuable. Roberto thought we'd getter a better price for it there and a friend had given him the name of a specialist dealer.'

'Yes, I know all about that.' I said, cutting in.

'You know?!' Mother replied incredulously, and I explained what had happened.

'Interpol are looking for a Signor Brighella.' I said pointedly, looking at Roberto.

'E allora?! They never catch me. Sono cretini!' Roberto laughed.

'Well, to finish the story...' Mother continued. 'After Amsterdam, we drove to Italy and stored the paintings in the basement of Roberto's antique shop in Treviso. We've sold a few, but most, being of great value of course, posed more of a problem.'

'Yes, I understand.'

'Roberto knew of Count Bolani and that he was a collector of eighteenth-century Italian paintings and an extremely wealthy man. He thought he might be interested. So we made an appointment with him and brought the Longhi paintings for him to view.

'I had no idea that he knew Theo and Bernard Skelton. Of course, he recognised the paintings and knew that they had belonged to Theo, a bequest under Sir Bernard's Will.

'I tried to bluff my way out of it, but the Count is too clever for that and he is a man of honour too. He saw through me, and in the end I had to tell him the whole story. He was very understanding, but made it clear that I had a duty to return the paintings and reconcile myself with you. If I didn't then, though he much regretted it, he would have no alternative but to inform the Carabinieri. The invitation to the Ball was his clever suggestion as a means of discreetly bringing us together, and here we are!'

'Yes, so we are indeed, but didn't you get my voicemail message asking you to call me?'

'No, I didn't answer either the phone or the mobile. In fact, I left my mobile in the bedroom at Orchard House.'

'I see. Tell me was it you, Mum, who followed me through the streets of Venice yesterday?'

'I'm afraid it was. I so wanted to say something to you, but I owed it to the Count to keep to his plan, the street would have been the wrong place, and this has been the better way...William, my darling, I feel so ashamed at what I have done. I'm so sorry.'

The Count, who had been quiet until now, looked towards me.

'William, if I may now call you that now, I'm sorry that my letter to you was not entirely truthful but the deception was in a good cause. Now, William, will you forgive your mother?'

'Of course, I will.' I said, and I had just begun to thank the Count for everything he'd done and for all his kindness, when the door of the library was suddenly flung open.

Two flunkies came in dragging between them a girl dressed as Arlecchina, the female version of Harlequin. There was a rapid exchange in Italian between the flunkies and the Count.

'Well, well' said the Count, turning to us 'It seems we have – what is it in English? – a gatecrasher! They tell me she knows you, William.'

The girl removed her mask. It was Tina.

'Tina, what on earth are you doing here?' I said, quite flabbergasted.

'Well,' she said 'I just had to come, to see that you were all right, and, well, just to see you. We were not too busy in the school office and the bursar let me have a few days off. I managed to get a cheap flight and book an Airbnb place near the station. The owner is a very nice lady and she fixed me up with this funny costume.'

'So this is Tina.' My mother said – odd, as I hadn't mentioned her.

'Tina, let me introduce my mother.'

'Your Mother?! I...I...don't understand'

'Don't worry. It's a long story; I'll explain it all later.'

'I've heard all about you, Tina my dear.' My mother said 'It's very nice to meet you, a most unexpected pleasure.'

'But, Mum, how do you know about Tina?'

'Ah, well, William, you see, when I said I wanted to draw a line under my old life, I didn't mean that I didn't want to know what was going on back home. You know my best friend from the Bridge Club, Vera Johnson?'

'Of course, we've met several times at Orchard House, and she came to the inquest.'

'Well, Vera knows about all this, I simply couldn't keep her in the dark about my plans and about Roberto, could I? She's the only one though, apart from Liam of course, and she acts as my spy, discreetly keeping me abreast of things at home.

'Vera is friendly with Wanda Parker, who, we all know, is a bit of a chatterbox. Wanda, who knows nothing I should add, told her all about you and Tina and that's how I come to know. And now here is Tina in person! William, I can see for myself now that she's a very nice girl, just as I knew she would be, and an extremely attractive one, too. You're a very lucky man.'

Tina beamed. She had never looked more beautiful.

'Don't you have something to say to Tina, William?' Mother asked, with a knowing motherly look.

'Oh, yes, I...I have' I said, turning to face Tina.

'Tina,' I continued, 'Do you think you might possibly...?'

'Marry you? Yes, I'd like that very much.' Tina replied, quickly, with a lovely smile.

'Well,' said the noble Count, beaming broadly 'I think this calls for Champagne!'

CHAPTER TWENTY-SEVEN

At dead of night, Roberto removed my father's paintings from the basement of his shop and deposited them a few miles to the north of Treviso in a derelict warehouse building which had belonged to a bankrupt company. They were found the next morning by the police following an anonymous telephone tip-off – Roberto with a scarf over his mouth.

I spent Ash Wednesday wandering, as if in a delightful dream, around Venice with Tina, my mother and Roberto, and the next day flew home to England. By a happy chance, Tina was booked on a flight departing shortly after mine.

'I don't want to raise your hopes too much' she said, as we waited in the departure lounge, 'but I've just had a text from a little bird in the school office, actually a big bird: Wanda in fact. She says that she overheard the Headmaster talking to the Bursar and there might be a letter waiting for you when you get home.'

We'd planned to spend the night at Tina's flat, but I dropped by mine on the way, and sure enough, amongst the post, was an envelope with the school crest. I sat down to read the enclosed letter from the Headmaster:

Dear *William*,

It gives me the greatest of pleasure to offer, on behalf of the school, to re-engage you as a History teacher with effect from the beginning of next term. Your salary will be based on that for last year but subject to an uplift of three per centum. If, as I hope, you are able to accept, the Bursar will write to you with a new employment contract for signature.

The proposed merger with Mallory College will not now

proceed, and the temporary arrangements between our two schools implemented this term in anticipation of the merger will cease as from the end of term, save for an informal understanding in respect of the shared use of certain sporting facilities.

I am sure that you will be as relieved as I am that Hanfield Manor will now be able to continue as an independent school and would wish to know the circumstances which have made this happy outcome possible.

A short while ago, we received a very generous private donation. The sum involved, I can assure you, is more than sufficient to restore the health of the school's balance sheet at least for long enough to allow time to implement the radical new business plan prepared by the Bursar.

The donor, Mrs. Stearnley-Owen, is an old friend of Sir Giles Pendleton, the Chairman of Governors, and I understand, that by chance, you have actually enjoyed the privilege of meeting her yourself whilst staying near Dulverton during the Christmas holidays. She is a truly remarkable woman of great intellect and charm and, moreover, she is acquainted with many powerful and influential people at the highest levels of society.

On Sir Giles' recommendation, Mrs. Stearnley-Owen has been appointed a Governor of the school. She is clearly a woman of old-fashioned moral values. In particular she believes in the virtue of strong discipline and has even advocated the re-introduction of the cane for bad behaviour. Her presence on the Board of Governors will, I'm sure, be a great asset to the school. William, you have been much missed by both staff and pupils, and will, I know, receive the warmest of welcomes on your return. I look forward to hearing from you.

Yours sincerely,
Hugh Drabble
Headmaster

CHAPTER TWENTY-EIGHT

Of course, I accepted the school's offer to re-engage me as a teacher at Hanfield Manor and returned to the job I have always loved.

Save for one or two works which we retained for sentimental reasons, all my father's paintings were sold at auction apart from the set of Longhi paintings, which the Count himself bought from us by way of private sale. He deserved to have them and he paid, without quibble, a very good price determined by an independent expert. It was sad to let the Longhis go, but Tina and I have a standing invitation to visit the Ca' Bolani whenever we travel to Venice and I shall be able to see them again and again in their beautiful new setting.

After paying inheritance tax and costs, there remained a very considerable sum for us to share. With part of the money, I was able to purchase Orchard House from Maurice Beckman & partners and I now live there in blissful contentment with Tina and a mischievous tabby cat called Brighella. Under the terms of the deal, I agreed to grant a lease-back to Beckmans of the ground floor gallery for which they pay me a handsome rent. I allowed my mother to keep all the rest of the money raised by the sales.

All the Delftware pieces, which had belonged to my father, were returned to me and, in turn, I returned them to Lotte Van de Groot, the proprietor of the shop in Amsterdam, who had originally bought them. Godfrey Bull, who had by chance seen and identified them as being the property of my father, later himself acquired an interest in the collection. This happened not by purchase but by the simple expedient of Godfrey marrying Lotte, whose capacious bosom he had always so much admired and for whom it transpired he had long nurtured a secret love. On his marriage, he had moved from Bath to Amsterdam to share Lotte's spacious flat in a lovely canal side house in the Leidsegracht, where their joint collection of old

Delftware, including my father's, is proudly displayed.

My mother declined to return to England. She felt she could hardly now 'come back from the dead' as Mrs. Wilkins. Instead she stayed in Italy and quietly married Roberto Trevisan. I had no objection to the marriage as I'd come to like and admire Roberto and believed that mother would be very happy with him. Tina and I are regular visitors to their elegant, sunny apartment in Treviso overlooking the river.

Finally, and best of all, Tina and I were married. The wedding was celebrated during the Easter holidays in the following year at the English Church of St Giles's in Venice in the Campo San Vio. The Count, who attended the wedding, very kindly allowed us to hold our reception in the magnificent ballroom of the Ca' Bolani.

A large contingent of friends and relatives, young and old, travelled from England for the occasion.

These included of course my aunt, Silly Milly, who wore what they call 'a fascinator', a ridiculous item of headgear which kept falling off and eventually blew away into a canal.

Uncle Charles was there and spent much of the reception eying up the ladies and telling rather questionable jokes.

Naturally, my old friends, Mike and Geoff, had come along.

Mike was accompanied by his new girlfriend, an attractive, lively girl who had recently been appointed as junior matron at the school. She is as keen as Mike on outdoor pursuits and sport, and they look as if they were well suited to one another. Perhaps, this time he will strike lucky.

Geoff came with Wanda in tow, or perhaps it was the other way round. Wanda had paid for first class flights for them both and a luxury double room booked at the famous Hotel Danieli. Apart from attending the wedding service and reception, I don't suppose Geoff saw much of Venice as he would have had other duties, as it were, to perform ('Well, it beats jogging' as he said later). I have a feeling that Geoff has quietly become rather fond of Wanda, and they seem very happy together.

Just as the wedding service was about to commence, a tall, elegantly dressed lady entered the church and sat by herself near the door. She was wearing one of those hats with a veil covering her face. But I knew who she was, and so did Count Bolani.

Fate, having done its worst and its best, had now departed, quietly closing the door behind it.

My metaphorical lift had finally ascended to the penthouse suite.

As those famous *they* would say, echoing the title of the Bard's play:

All's Well That Ends Well.

Lightning Source UK Ltd.
Milton Keynes UK
UKOW05f1232220916

283502UK00008B/188/P